DISTINGUISHED BUMPKIN

SAM CHEEVER

ELECTRIC PROSE PUBLICATIONS

PRAISE FOR SAM CHEEVER

"You have that essential Je ne sais quoi that it takes to tell a story so mesmerizing you cannot stop reading once started. You are not telling stories to your readers...you are taking them with you on your adventures so that the experience can be shared by all as it happens and not simply replayed like a memory on the page of a diary! You are indeed gifted and it is my pleasure to read your books!"

Valerie Irwin

Deer Hollow's new mayor has a past. He portrays himself as a distinguished member of the community. But Joey isn't buying what he's selling. It might have something to do with the dead body draped over his breakfast table.

Lord Acton once said, "Power corrupts, and absolute power corrupts absolutely."

I wouldn't know. I have no power.

My name is Joey and I'm an unabashed bumpkin. I live in a quaint and quirky country town named Deer Hollow. We're pretty simple and laid back in the Hollow. But that doesn't mean the occasional murder can't happen here. It's just that when it does, it seems more surprising somehow.

Especially when a corpse turns up in the mayor's kitchen.

(Psst! If you're keeping track, *he* does have power.)

But don't worry, we're on it. By "we" I mean me, the Greek deity (my boyfriend Hal), and my sweet Pitbull Caphy. Yeah, I didn't include my snooty Siamese cat, LaLee or our adorable pot-bellied pig Ethel Squeaks. Not because I love them any less. But let's face it, the cat isn't going to get her paws dirty delving into a messy murder, and the pig... well...she tends to hoard all the evidence in her little tent in my kitchen, so...

STAY IN TOUCH

Sam doesn't give away a lot of books. But she values her readers and, to show it, she's gifting you a copy of a fun book just for signing up for her newsletter!

SIGN UP HERE!
https://samcheever.com/newsletter/

1

I stood in the shade of an enormous ash tree and sipped a fruity drink my PI had handed me before disappearing into the crowd. In the distance, I could easily see his midnight black head above all the others and wondered who he was talking to.

He'd tried to get me to work the crowd with him, but I'll admit, I still had a bad taste in my mouth for the new mayor.

I didn't like it when people did despicable things and got away with it. In Mayor Robb's case, he'd managed to blame his wife for his own crimes, which had been easy to do since she'd done some pretty despicable things too. Because of her, a kind young woman had died. And I'd been drawn into the murder through a strange composite of events and happenstance.

I did blame the mayor for what his wife had done. That might seem unfair on the surface. But his actions had inspired hers, and lots of people, and one cranky Siamese cat, had suffered for it.

"Joey?"

I turned to find a pretty blonde woman heading my way, a smile on her face. Cecily Addams reached a hand toward me as she approached and pulled me into a hug. "I'm so glad to see a friendly face."

"Hey, Cecily. It's nice to see you again." I knew how she felt. I didn't know most of the people at the garden party. I assumed most of them were donors from Indianapolis and the surrounding area. Mayor Robb might have only been the mayor of a small town in bumpkinville, but he had friends in influential places and was just about as ambitious as they came.

"Where's that gorgeous boyfriend of yours?"

"He's schmoozing." I nodded toward Hal, who'd moved farther away and was talking to Sheriff Mulhern at the edge of the party. The sheriff was one of the reasons we were there. Hal depended on the Deer Hollow sheriff's department for business so he could justify spending half his time with me in the Hollow.

He and his brother Cal Amity had a PI business based in Indianapolis. But Hal had started a bumpkin office, picking up business not only from Deer Hollow but all the surrounding towns too.

Cecily groaned. "I should be chatting up the donors myself. I just can't seem to find the energy."

"I don't know how you do it," I commiserated. "After everything that's happened..." I didn't need to elaborate. Cecily had lost a dear friend as a result of the Robbs' dirty dealings.

She grimaced. "I'm doing the least I can get away with. Benson and I have something in the works. As soon as we get to the point where I can leave, I'm gone."

Benson Dexter was Cecily's boyfriend and also just

happened to have been the mayor's biggest competition in his run for office. "Oh?" I gave her my best small-town gossip look. "Do tell."

She laughed. "You'll be one of the first to know when we're ready."

I squeezed her arm. "Does this mean you two are sticking around?"

Cecily slid a contemplative look around the party, her expression serious. "When Martin Robb told me he was running for office down here and wanted my help, my first thought was to decline. I've never lived in a rural area. I thought I'd hate it. But I've found it strangely..." She seemed to be foraging for the right word.

"Refreshing?"

Her lips curved in a genuine smile. "That's a perfect word for it. Benson has gone through the same metamorphosis. Despite the trouble with Robb, he's fallen in love with this area."

"How's he doing? I haven't seen him since he was exonerated."

"He's good. He's been working hard on that new enterprise I told you about. We both have."

"Good. Caphy loves him, and that definitely means something in my book."

She laughed. "Well, your sweet girl inspired him too. I'm happy to say we're now the proud parents of two sweet and beautiful rescue pups."

I squealed happily and pulled her into a hug. "Congratulations, fur mama."

She laughed. "It is a lot like being a mom, isn't it?"

"It is. Except they can't really talk back." I frowned as soon as I said the words, thinking of all the ways my three furbabies did just that. I sighed. "I take that back. They do that too."

Cecily laughed. "I'd love for you to meet them. Maybe, when things calm down a bit, we can have you and Hal over for dinner."

"We'd love that."

Another squeal brought my head whipping around. All heads turned to take in my bestie Lis as she hurried toward me, her handsome boyfriend in tow.

Deputy Arno Willager, Deer Hollow's favorite villager, as Lis liked to call him, looked about as thrilled to be at the garden party as we were.

Lis wrapped her slender arms around me in a hug. "Hey, you! I'm so happy to see you here. I thought I was going to have to navigate this nightmare all by myself."

"I'm standing right here," Arno objected with one brow peaked.

Lis laughed. "You don't count. You're going to have to schmooze with your horrible boss the whole time."

Arno lowered his voice as heads turned our way. "Ix-nay on the orrible-hay."

We laughed.

"Oh. Have you two met Cecily?" I asked.

They exchanged polite greetings and handshakes.

"She's Mayor Robb's assistant..."

"Speaking of horrible bosses," Cecily murmured.

Lis barked out a laugh. "I'm going to like you," she told my new friend.

"She's hiding here with us," I told Lis. "We're starting a new club."

Nodding, Cecily added, "Our superpower is snob avoidance."

"We'll hide in the shade and drink frou-frou drinks," Lis said. "I love it."

Arno cast a doleful glance toward Sheriff Mulhern, who'd ditched Hal and was networking with donors. "I want to be part of your club."

I patted his muscular shoulder. "Sorry, you have to go hob nob with a snob."

We giggled like idiots as Arno rolled his eyes. "Fine. I see how you are." He gave Lis a quick kiss on the cheek. "I'll be back soon. I'm only going to do the bare minimum in snob-hobnobbing."

We watched him head into the fray with heavy steps. He'd barely moved fifteen feet away before someone hailed him, and he was drawn into what was likely a painful conversation. For Arno, the event was more an opportunity for people to blame him for not stopping everything that went wrong within a hundred-mile radius of Deer Hollow. There was no way he could win at that game.

"This cabin is amazing," Lis said.

Cecily nodded. "I took a quick tour before I came outside. It is stunning."

"You haven't seen it yet?" I asked Lis. "You were his realtor for the property, weren't you?"

"I helped the Mayor buy the land, but I hadn't seen the house."

We all turned to look at the ridiculously oversized log cabin, which, if the rumors were correct, was over seven thousand square feet of pure opulence and pretentiousness.

"I've been dying to go inside," I admitted.

Cecily took the drink from my hand and threw it on the ground. "Oh my," she said as I barked out a laugh. "It looks like you need a new glass. Come with me. I know exactly where we can get you one inside the house."

"What if we get caught?" Lis asked.

Cecily glanced pointedly toward the spot at the edge of the party, where Robb was speaking to a beautiful woman with silver-white hair. They had their heads together and looked like they were whispering sweet promises into each other's ears. "I don't think he's even going to notice we're gone."

2

We clung to the shadows at the front of the house, all but skulking from bush to bush like comic book villains in our attempt to stay unnoticed.

Cecily had assured us we wouldn't get into trouble for snooping. Mayor Robb loved to show off his new home. But if our new vocation was to avoid talking to political types, being discovered sneaking into the house was a sure way to ruin our day.

Cecily led us to the side door, which she said would take us into a mudroom and down a hallway to the kitchen.

"Won't there be catering staff in there?" Lis asked.

She nodded. "There might be. But the food prep staff is gone, and all that's left are the serving staff. Most of them are hanging out around the bars and the buffet table on the patio. They only come inside to get ice and replenish the alcohol stores. I've been to parties with this group before, they don't eat much, but they go through an incredible amount of alcohol."

Lis laughed. "I can see why. I'd drink too much too if I had to socialize with that group."

Cecily nodded. She pulled open a heavy oak door with a frosted glass panel in its center and ushered us inside ahead of her.

We stepped into a large mudroom, whose floors were wide planks of golden wood and whose walls held built-in shelves, nooks, and cabinets painted a glossy white. A work jacket and a black cap with the mayor's office logo on it hung on hooks immediately inside the door. A pair of boots sat on a raised shelf below them.

When we stepped into the hall, we were met with the sweet, fresh smell of cedar, accompanied by the scents of the food Robb was serving to his guests. Despite my desire to dislike the man, I had to admit he'd done a great job with the house.

The walls were painted a creamy white, but the trim and high ceilings looked like raw cedar that appeared to be oiled rather than stained. Thick, off-white rugs made the walk down the long hallway feel luxurious.

There was a closed door along the way that Cecily told us was the laundry room. Ahead of us, at the end of the hall, was an enormous room with cedar walls and wide plank floors. The room was outfitted with comfortable yet masculine gray leather couches and contrasting chairs of creamy yellow leather.

Seeing the long wall of floor-to-ceiling built-in bookshelves, I longed to explore the space, but Cecily pointed to a wide opening on our right, and we turned into a kitchen that was nearly as big as the entire first floor of my house.

My first thought was that it was a professional kitchen. It was the kitchen of a man who intended to entertain often and not do the cooking himself. It had clearly been built to accommodate the type of crew that was catering the party outside.

My second thought was that I'd kill for the retro-style appliances, with their rounded, nostalgic lines and over-the-moon coolness factor.

My third thought was that the man who was draped over the small table in the cozy little nook built into the corner didn't really go with the rest of the décor.

Especially since he seemed to be bleeding all over the gorgeous, white marble floor.

Shrill, panicked screaming pierced my thoughts and the silence.

I looked from Cecily to Lis and frowned, realizing my two stoic companions weren't the ones who were screaming. Cecily had lost a few shades of color. She was also bug-eyed, and she was breathing too fast. Lis's beautiful face had a "not again" expression on it. She cast me a slightly accusing glance, and I fought the desire to defend myself.

The screaming gained in pitch, and all three of our gazes slid toward a young woman dressed in black slacks and a pristine white blouse, who'd apparently just emerged from the butler's pantry at the side of the room.

The woman's gaze slipped from me to the dead man, to Lis, back to the dead man, and then to Cecily, whom she appeared to recognize and seemed to immediately count as suspect due to her proximity to us. The server's scream never abated through the entire two minutes it took for the rest of the party to join us.

When Cecily took a step in her direction, arm outstretched as if she wanted to offer sympathy, the young server's fingers relaxed, and she dropped an entire case of amber liquid onto the floor. Glass and liquid flew every-where, and the strong scent of whiskey filled the room.

The woman then turned and ran back into the pantry, slamming the door behind her. The screaming continued from the other side of the door, though thankfully slightly muffled.

Lis and I and Cecily looked at each other, and Cecily sighed. "So much for sneaking into the house unnoticed."

"We should call the police," Lis said, eyeing the corpse with surprising calm.

"The police are right outside," I reminded her.

She grimaced. "I suppose they're going to think we killed him."

Cecily's eyes went wide. "Do you think?"

I shrugged. "Mayor Robb doesn't like me very much. I'm sure he'll try to pin it on me."

That, actually, was a pretty big understatement.

We stood there for a long moment in silence, each of us caught up in our own thoughts.

Cecily looked from me to Lis. "You two are taking this really calmly."

I shrugged. "This is like my tenth dead body. I think I'm getting numb."

Lis nodded. "I think I'm getting vicariously numb through Joey. Plus, I survived the cutthroat world of model-ing. I'm pretty sure that made me immune to anything except the most violent kind of event."

Cecily nodded thoughtfully.

"What about you?" I said. "You're handling it better than most people would."

She snorted out a laugh that had nothing to do with humor. "I deal with politicians every day. You could probably drive a stake through my skin, and I wouldn't even feel it."

I chuckled, understanding completely.

Then, I sighed. "I guess we'd better go get Arno before that poor woman in there does damage to herself."

The server was still shrieking as if someone was yanking her fingernails out one by one.

LIS, Cecily, and I stood as far away from the group by the table as possible. I tried to make myself really small and disappear into the woodwork. Or, failing that, into the next room, if possible.

Mayor Robb kept flinging death glares in my direction as if it was my fault a dead guy ended up on his kitchen table.

Granted, Martin Robb and I both knew I didn't like him. We both knew the feeling was mutual. But only one of us believed that I'd resort to murder to get rid of Deer Hollow's duly elected mayor.

Cecily slid me a look of pity. "Wow, he really doesn't like you."

I chewed the inside of my lip.

"He blames her for that whole mess last month, which he totally got himself into, by the way," Lis said in my defense.

I bumped shoulders with her. "Thanks for the trust and support. It appears to be in short supply right now."

Standing near the doorway to the butler's pantry, Arno fixed me with a glare over the head of the woman he was interviewing. It was the shrieking server from before. She kept throwing accusatory looks our way as she answered his questions, leaving me to wonder what horrible things she was telling the deputy.

Even Hal, standing near the corpse with the sheriff, was throwing me speculative looks. I fought the urge to shrug and look innocent.

"Why does everybody think I killed this guy?" I murmured to myself.

I must have spoken louder than intended because Lis put an arm around my shoulders and gave me a squeeze. Even in her leather flats, my bestie towered over my five foot four inches. She was tall and slim and, even in the throes of becoming a murder suspect, she was impossibly beautiful in a plain cotton sundress that hugged her curves and flared out a couple of inches above her knees to showcase perfect legs.

Beside her, I felt like the ugly bumpkin, despite the fact that I was wearing my favorite summer dress and pretty white sandals. My strawberry-blonde hair curled around my shoulders, slightly frizzy in the humidity but mostly behaving for once. A sheen of sweat covered my face, and my stomach gurgled with nerves. I was starting to understand why Arno didn't want me anywhere near his murder investigations. Not only was I approaching a professional level in finding bodies, but I had a tendency to draw killers like bees to the queen.

Arno patted the distraught server on the arm and turned toward our little group. He stopped to let the guys with the gurney past before fixing a laser gaze on us and heading our way with long, angry strides.

He didn't even look at Lis when he approached. His gaze was locked on me. Still, he hadn't completely gone over to the dark side. He kept his voice low when he started berating me. "Why do I think you're behind this?"

I felt my eyes go wide. "You think I killed that guy?"

His brown eyes narrowed accusingly. "Of course not. But if you hadn't been snooping where you don't belong, you'd have never put all of us into this position."

Okay, that did it. "*All* of us? Exactly how have I inconvenienced you? Maybe you should stop browbeating me and focus on finding the guy who *really* caused this problem. The killer."

Arno lowered his head and his voice. "The sheriff is talking about removing all citizen consultants from the payroll. Between what happened last month and now, with you popping up in the middle of another murder, you may have just single-handedly cost Hal his gig and lost me a valuable asset."

"That's not fair," Lis objected.

Arno made a motion for her to keep her voice low.

She glared at him in a way that told me he wasn't going to be enjoying girlfriend bennies anytime soon. "Joey's not any more at fault for this than she was for the last mess the mayor got himself into. If you're looking for a scapegoat, then you don't need to be looking for it anywhere around my friends or me."

Arno paled slightly beneath his tan, but he pinched his lips together and shook his head. "Melissa, you need to stay out of this and let me do my job."

Oh, no, he din'nt!

Lis stiffened, her beautiful face turning red. "Did you just call me Melissa?"

He had. And I could tell from the look of horror on his face that he realized just how big a mistake that was. Nobody was really sure why, but Lis had always hated her real name. Something about having been named after a crazy great-aunt with a penchant for coyote-ugly type bar behavior. And she especially hated when someone used it in a chastising tone as Arno just had. Nobody with a lick of sense did that.

Arno was toast.

"Cecily?" Mayor Robb called from across the room. When she looked at him, he jerked his head to summon her over.

She and I shared a commiserating look. I watched her join her boss and then, after a brief, low-voiced conversation, follow his stiff, angry strides out of the room.

Hal joined me as Lis stormed from the room, leaving a grim Arno behind. When the cop glowered in my direction, I glared right back. "Don't try to blame me for any of this, Arno Willager. All I did was come into the kitchen for a drink of water and a peek at the house. I didn't have anything to do with that poor man on the table."

Arno sighed. "I need to take your statement. Do you want me to come by your place later?"

"That will be fine," I said, my tone clipped. I was sorry for the man who was being loaded onto a stretcher for a ride to the morgue. Very sorry. And I was sorry that Arno was on the hot seat again, with both the mayor and his girlfriend. But neither of those things were my fault, and I was tired of being treated as if they were.

Hal took my arm, urging me toward the door. "Let's go home. We need to feed Ethel Squeaks anyway."

"Doesn't Arno need your help?"

Hal shook his head. "Let's go."

"But..."

He fixed an intense look on me. "Joey, let's go. I'll explain later."

His message was clear. There were things going on that I

didn't know about. Again. And he couldn't tell me about them until we were alone.

"Okay." I let him slip his fingers through mine and gratefully left the big fancy house behind.

3

"It's just really bad timing," my PI told me as we drove toward home. "Mayor Robb's been chirping in the sheriff's ear to get rid of me anyway."

I tensed with righteous anger on Hal's behalf. He was a darn good PI, and he'd been a huge help to Arno on the cases they'd worked together. "That's just wrong. You're saving him tons of money because he doesn't have to hire more deputies. He should be grateful."

Hal's smile was grim. "He doesn't quite see it that way, honey."

"It's because I came forward with evidence against him in the Kat Leonard case, isn't it?"

"I'm not going to lie, Joey. That didn't help."

I chewed my lip. "Okay, I'll take the hit for that. But I honestly don't know what else I could have done."

He reached over and clasped my hand in a big, warm grip, squeezing it. "You couldn't have done anything else. Robb's dirty. We all know it. But he also got really lucky because it was easy to pin everything on his wife. Eventually, his luck's going to run out." Hal's hand on the steering wheel tightened, showing white knuckles. "I'm going to make sure of that."

"Are you shut out of this case?" I asked, feeling better.

"Not yet. Arno and I will keep my contribution to the investigation quiet. But, even if the sheriff says I'm out, I'll keep working it. I just need someone to hire me to investigate."

I grinned. "If that happens, I have a dollar bill with your name on it."

Hal laughed. "You really know how to dazzle a guy. How could I turn that down?"

"You're worth every penny. Besides, there are perks."

He waggled his dark brows at me, and it was my turn to laugh. "Get your mind out of the sewer, Amity. I was talking about the pibl and banana cream pie."

"I knew that."

"Mm-hm." I chuckled. "I'll even let you buy me that pie. That's just the kind of girl I am."

"How did I get so lucky?"

"I have no idea."

Arno looked beat when he finally arrived at my house two hours later. I felt bad for him. He'd really needed the day off, and a party with Lis on his arm had been just the ticket until it had all gone haywire in a most spectacular way.

"Have you ID'd the victim?" I asked as I handed Arno a cup of coffee.

"Yeah. He's the owner of the catering company for the party." Arno sipped his coffee and lowered himself wearily to a stool. "This tastes great. Thanks, Joey."

"It's the least I can do," I told him with a guilty smile.

"I'm sorry I found another body and wrecked your pseudo day off."

Arno shook his head. "Obviously, it's not your fault." He looked up from his mug. "Unless you killed him?"

"Why do I detect a hopeful note in your question?" I asked, laughter in my voice.

"I'd be sad to put you in prison. And I'm sure Amity would miss you." He shrugged, his lips twitching. "But if you confessed, I could close the case and go try to make up with my girlfriend."

I barked out a laugh. "Sorry to disappoint. And, just FYI, the full name thing with Lis is on a level with murder in her book. Her mother used to crank it out whenever she was trying to get Lis's goat. Lis hates it."

"It's a dumb thing to get so riled up about," he groused.

I shuddered. "Good heavens, man! Don't let Lis hear you say that, or the road back will be long, twisty, and filled with man-eating potholes."

Hal chuckled. "This is why somebody wrote the book about women being from Venus." When I threw him a glare, he quickly said. "As a Martian, I'm sure all we're dealing with is a cultural difference." He patted Arno on the shoulder. "And we all know that the best way to make it up to a Venetian is to prostrate ourselves before them and declare our complete idiocy."

"Don't forget chocolate," I added helpfully.

Arno didn't seem even a tiny bit amused by our banter. "If we could get back to the case?"

Shrugging, I said, "It's your funeral. Romantically speaking."

He sighed. "Robb has no idea why someone would stab the caterer in his kitchen. Except for a five-minute lapse when he disappeared into the house to take a call in private,

Robb has the very best alibi there is. He was within eyesight of the sheriff and me the whole time."

"Five minutes is plenty of time to stab a guy and return to the party," I said helpfully.

"Yes," Arno agreed. "But why? He has no obvious motive, and it was a real buzzkill on the party."

"What did the woman you spoke to in the kitchen have to say?" I asked.

Arno frowned. "The server?"

I nodded.

"She was pretty upset..."

"Yeah, I noticed," I said, wincing.

"We don't have an easily discernable motive for her. Other than stepping into the butler's pantry to grab supplies, she didn't leave her station all afternoon."

"She didn't notice the body when she came into the kitchen?" I asked. "How is that possible?"

Arno shook his head. "She says no. And given how she was shrieking, I'm guessing she's telling the truth."

"Or she was putting on a really good act," I said.

"Did you see him right away?" he asked, narrowing his gaze on me.

I thought about it and then shook my head. "Not right away, but within a few seconds." The table he'd been draped over was tucked into a little alcove that looked out over the backyard. It was easy to see if someone stood in the doorway and looked around as we had. But if you hurried in and went straight to the pantry. "I guess it's possible she missed him."

Arno nodded. "That's what I was thinking. Have you ever heard of a phenomenon called hyperfocus?"

I shook my head.

"It's a real thing. When somebody is really concentrating

on a task, their brain shuts out everything around them. We see it all the time from victims of a crime. They're so focused on what's happening to them, they could literally walk right past an enormous pink elephant and not see it."

"Like tunnel vision?" I asked.

He nodded.

"But that generally happens under extreme stress situations," Hal noted.

Shrugging, Arno said. "This was the young woman's first week on a new job. She was nervous about screwing up. She desperately needs to keep the job with the caterer. Everybody's stress initiators are different."

I wasn't ready to discount the server yet. If she'd killed the caterer and then heard us coming, she might have ducked into the pantry so she could pretend she'd been there all along. "Did she have any blood on her?"

Arno shook his head. "Not that I could see. But there wouldn't have been any spray. He was only stabbed once. Castoff generally comes from a follow-up strike."

"What about the weapon?" Hal asked.

"Regular kitchen knife. Big, with a serrated edge. It appears to have come right out of the knife block on the center island."

Which meant it likely hadn't been premeditated.

"Do we have a TOD?" Hal asked.

"He'd been dead for less than an hour. In fact, he was still warm."

In my humble opinion, that news made it seem even more likely the server was the killer.

"We need to find out more about this Jonathan Calliente," Arno told Hal. "Clients, finances, friends, enemies. We need to figure out if he was the intended target or if he'd just been in the wrong place at the wrong time."

Hal nodded. "I'll get started on that right away."

Arno stood, rubbing a hand over his face. "I have about a hundred party-goers to interview. Wish me luck."

"You're going back to the party?" Hal asked, surprised.

"No." He frowned. "Robb insisted his guests be allowed to leave. Sheriff Mulhern backed him up. So now we get to contact each of them individually and interview them on their own turf. Robb just added days of legwork to our investigation."

I bit my lip to keep from asking if I was allowed to help with the investigation, preferring to fall back on the "what Arno doesn't know won't hurt him" defense. I was pretty sure the last investigation, the one I was supposed to stay as far away from as humanly possible, had finally cemented the "Joey's going to end up entangled in the case anyway, so we might as well embrace it" rule.

Still, I didn't want to push my luck.

4

We entered Sonny's Diner a couple of hours later and stood at the door looking around the crowded restaurant. The owner, Max, waved at us from the order window, pointing to a booth in front of the window. "I'll be there as soon as I can," she called over the noise of lively conversation.

I waved back, giving her a thumbs up. Hal placed a hand in the small of my back, gently nudging me forward. I saw why a beat later, when the door flew open and two men in ball caps stumbled in, swearing loudly and laughing. The smell of sour alcohol wafted over us, and I wrinkled my nose.

Sliding into the indicated booth, I grimaced at the stickiness of the table. I looked around for Jimmy, the busboy, but he was nowhere in sight.

Max sent the rowdy drunks toward the counter with a glare and hurried over to us, her face flushed and glistening from her activity. She shook her head, flinging a rag down on the table. "I'll tell you what. It never fails," she groused, handing us our menus. "There's some kind of flu going

around town, and both Jimmy and Verna are at home sick."
She shoved a frizzy strand of yellow-white hair off her face.
"So, of course, half the town decides it's a good night to
come in."

I looked around the place, seeing a number of tables
with no food and a few vying desperately for Max's attention. "Do you have someone else you can call?"

Max sighed, looking older than her fifty-some years.
"No. Everybody's either sick or on vacation." She shook her
head and tugged her order pad out of her apron. "I'll
survive. Dinner just might be a bit slow tonight. I'm missing
cooks too."

I looked at Hal and he nodded. I shoved to my feet.
"What can we do to help?"

Max started to reject my offer and then stopped. "You
know what? If you're serious about helping, I'd really appreciate it. Can you take some orders and cart some food
for me?"

"I'd love to."

"Where do you need me?" Hal asked.

Max narrowed her gaze on him. "Can you cook?"

"I can take direction with the best of them."

"He's being modest. He's a great cook," I told Max.

"Good. Poor Tom is overwhelmed back there. Two of our
cooks called in sick, and Tom's been here since seven this
morning. If you could help him, I'd really appreciate it."

Hal touched her shoulder. "You got it." He strode toward
the swinging door and disappeared into the kitchen.

Max looked at me. There were tears in her eyes. She
gave me a quick hug. "Thanks so much. I'll owe ya a big
one."

"Anytime," I said. "Just save us a slice of pie, and we'll be
even."

She laughed. "I'll save you a whole dang pie. Now, let's get you a pad and an apron."

"I SAID I didn't want peas," a cranky elderly woman I didn't know barked out. "They give me gas. I wanted the green beans."

I bit back a retort and apologized, grabbing the plate back. "I'm sorry. I'll go fix it."

"Miss!" I barely made it two steps before one of the pre-teens in booth four waved me over.

I forced myself to smile. "Yes?"

"We asked for catsup twenty minutes ago. Our fries are cold now. We want new fries."

I looked around the table and fought panic. Six plates with burgers and fries. I'd have to drop off the pea-phobic lady's plate and come back. It had been a long time since I'd hustled plates, and I wasn't sure I could carry six of them at once. That meant two trips, and my dogs were beyond tired.

Max came up behind me and handed the kids a bottle of catsup. "Stop torturing Joey," she told the complaining teen, glowering down at him. "Or I'll tell your mom I saw you kissing Missy Palentine outside the library last night."

The boy's pimply face paled, and he slumped in his seat.

I fought a grin. Whispering, "Thanks!" to Max, I hurried to the kitchen for a pea-extraction. Stopping in front of the pass-thru window, I was surprised to see Hal working the grill. "Where's Tom?"

Hal looked up, his handsome face flushed from the heat of the grill. His dark eyes twinkled as he looked at me. "Cigarette break out back. I think he's smoking a whole pack. He's been gone for a while."

I frowned. "You doing okay?"

He actually grinned. "I'm having a ball. Did I ever tell you I worked in a place a lot like this to put myself through college?"

"You did not." I grinned back. "But now that I know, I'm going to make you do all the cooking from now on."

He arched a midnight brow. "I already do all the cooking. Even, it seems, when we go out to eat."

I laughed. He wasn't wrong. "Can you swap out these peas for green beans, please?" I leaned in. "Peas give her gas." He grimaced and quickly made the switch. Handing it back to me, he said, "Even if Tom's heading for Mexico right now, I'd rather be back here than dealing with all those people out there."

"You have no idea," I whispered. "It's an angry crowd."

I took the plate back to the old woman. "Here you go."

"About time," she groused.

I turned away so I wouldn't say something about how rude she was. The booth nearest the door was empty, and the table was covered in dirty dishes. I went to get the bin and started filling it.

The door jangled, and I looked up to find a familiar face coming through the door. When the server from the mayor's house spotted me, she blanched, glancing at the door as if she was considering making a run for it.

I gave her a smile and picked up the now-full bin. "If you'll give me just a minute, I'll wipe this down and get you menus."

I hurried away, hoping she didn't leave. I'd love to question her about what she saw in that kitchen. When I returned, the woman was sitting down across from a dark-haired man who was around the same age. They were both wearing the white shirts and black trousers of the catering crew.

"Sorry," I said, offering another smile. "Apparently, there's a flu going around, and poor Max was short of help."

I handed them menus.

"You work here?" the woman asked, looking surprised.

"Just for tonight. What can I get you to drink?"

By the time I brought two sweet teas to the table, the couple was ready to order. I took their orders and hesitated. The woman's expression turned wary. "I'm sorry, I just wondered if you were doing okay? Finding that guy was..." I shuddered.

She chewed her bottom lip. "It was gruesome."

"Yes."

"You and your friends seemed pretty chill about it, though."

I wasn't sure how to respond. Telling her that I found bodies all the time probably wouldn't go over very well. I settled on, "We date cops." The truth. Sort of.

As if that explained everything, she nodded.

I offered my hand. "I'm Joey."

The woman shook it. "Karinne Magness." She nodded at her dinner companion. "That's Prince."

"Nice to meet you, Prince. I love your music," I quipped.

He gave me a flat stare in return. "Whatever."

Alrighty then. I nodded toward his clothes. "Looks like you worked the party too?"

"I did. I was on the dessert table."

"My favorite place," I said, grinning. Talking about food made my stomach rumble. I was really going to enjoy that banana cream pie Max had set aside for us.

He shrugged. Clearly, the guy had no sense of humor.

"It's quite a shock about your boss, huh?"

Karinne shuddered. Prince frowned at his silverware.

"Do you know of anybody who might have wanted him dead?"

Prince snorted. "That list is long. The guy was a jerk."

Karinne glared at him. "That's not fair, P. He was understandably nervous since the client threatened him like that."

My spidey senses perked. "Mayor Robb threatened Jonathan Calliente?"

Karinne looked irritated by my question. "I told that cop this."

I fought not to cringe. If she refused to tell me because she'd already told one of the deputies her story, there'd be nothing I could say to get her to open up. I couldn't exactly say I was a cop. Though, I might be able to throw the PI card at her.

Fortunately, I didn't need to go that far.

"The cop didn't seem all that interested. But I think it's important. Jon was a nervous wreck after the argument." She glanced at her companion. "He was a little short with everybody because of it."

"This was before the party?"

Shaking her head, Karinne clarified. "Just after it started, I guess. That woman got right in John's face and told him he'd never work in the area again. She said the mayor would see to that."

"What woman?"

"I don't know her name. The petite blonde. She works for the mayor. You know her. She was with you in the kitchen this afternoon."

I blinked. *Cecily?* "But you said the mayor threatened him."

Karinne gave me a sigh of exasperation. "She's the mayor's right hand, isn't she? You don't think a man like

Robb would do his own dirty work, do you? I've had experience with these politician types. Believe me, they're not going to stick their necks out. And they're used to taking what they want."

Karinne was bitter. That was obvious. I wondered what kind of experience she'd had. But I didn't want to get her off track by asking. Besides, she was right. I didn't think Robb did his own dirty work if he could help it. In fact, I knew he didn't. But what if the dirty work was Cecily's own? "Do you know what it was about?" I asked. "What did he do that made her threaten him?"

Karinne shook her head. "I have no idea. All I heard was her telling him he'd never get another job."

Prince fidgeted in his seat, drawing my gaze to his guilty face.

"What?" I asked. "Do you know something?"

The order pickup bell jangled. "Order, Joey," Hal called out.

Prince nudged Karinne's arm. "Come on, I'm not hungry anymore."

Not wanting to chase after them and cause a scene, I watched them walk out of Sonny's with a sinking feeling in my gut.

Prince knew something that might throw light on the murder. And I'd just lost my chance at finding out what.

"Jeezopete!" I said under my breath, heading to the window to pick up my order.

5

We finally trudged out of the diner at nine o'clock, carrying two chicken and noodle meals and a whole banana cream pie as promised.

Max, who didn't talk much in general, and was about as mushy as a rhinoceros, hugged us each and thanked us several times for the help, her eyes even getting misty.

I felt good about helping a friend. But exhausted down to my toes.

"Ethel Squeaks is going to think somebody cut her throat," Hal said.

I cringed at the saying. I'd never liked it. "She got a whole plate of fruit before we left. Even she can survive three hours without eating."

He opened the door of his big, black Escalade and gave me an assist when my tired body stuck midway climbing inside. "Ugh!" I said. "I feel like I'm fifty years old right now."

He tugged a messy strand of my strawberry blonde hair. "Just focus on the pie you're going to eat when we get home. It will help your old body keep functioning."

I grinned. "It might even give me a bounce in my step."

Chuckling, he closed the door and headed around to the driver's side.

I sagged into the leather beneath me. Nah. Who was I kidding? It would be a miracle if I managed to make it inside the house.

An hour later, sprawled on my couch with my feet in Hal's lap, I groaned happily as he rubbed my tired and swollen feet. Caphy, her muzzle still frothy with whipped cream from the tiny slice of pie I'd given her, had her big head resting on my shoulder, her pretty green gaze locked on my face. I told myself she was worried about me since I was a sugar-saturated puddle on the couch, but I was pretty sure she was just hoping I'd give in and offer her another slice of pie.

Ethel Squeaks was snorfling around in her little tent in the kitchen, no doubt preparing her nest for the night. She'd also enjoyed the pie. Though, in deference to her figure, we'd left the crust off her portion, giving her just filling and whipped cream.

She might have been squealing unhappily when we'd arrived home, but with her tummy filled and a cozy nest calling, she was as happy as a pig in a tent.

I groaned as Hal's thumbs found my arches. "That feels amazing."

He rested his head back and closed his eyes. "I have a new respect for people who work in a restaurant."

I nodded. "It's hard work." I eyed my PI. "I thought you worked in one during college?"

"I did," he agreed, fixing his dark green gaze on me. "But I was much younger then."

I laughed. He talked like he was forty instead of the strong, healthy thirty-two years he was.

Then I remembered what I'd learned about Cecily and pulled myself to a sitting position, dislodging the pibl from my shoulder. With a long-suffering sigh, Caphy circled three times and curled into a ball on the floor next to the couch.

Poor thing. She had to sleep on the floor like a dog rather than on the couch like the human she believed she was.

"I talked to that server from the party tonight."

Hal's eyes widened. "She was in Sonny's?"

I nodded. "Her and another one of the servers. His name is Prince. He's desserts."

"Your favorite."

I flashed him a quick grin. "Yes, well, *he's* not my favorite. He knows something about the victim he wouldn't tell me." I filled my PI in on what I'd learned, Hal's handsome face growing less weary as I talked.

"Cecily threatened the victim?"

"It looks that way."

He thought about that for a minute. "We need to talk to her and this Prince guy."

I nodded. "Karinne said Cecily threatened the man not too long after the party started. When we were talking about the house, Cecily told Lis and me that she'd been in there earlier. So she's not trying to hide the fact she was in there."

"It *would* be a pretty gutsy move to kill the man and then drag a bunch of witnesses to the crime scene," Hal said thoughtfully. "Especially after being overheard threatening the guy."

As much as I liked Cecily, I felt the need to play devil's advocate. "Unless she didn't know Karinne was eavesdropping. Caterers tend to blend into the scenery. They try to keep a low profile, so they don't intrude on clients and their company. Karinne could have been in the butler's pantry when Cecily was threatening him."

"True," Hal agreed. "And it would be gutsy but effective to uncover your own crime with witnesses who could attest to walking in with you and finding the body."

"We need to talk to that Prince guy and find out what he knows. I have a feeling he can shine some light on a possible motive for Jonathan Calliente's murder."

I WAS SITTING at the island drinking coffee and compiling a grocery list the next morning when the front door opened, and Lis called out to me. "In the kitchen!" I called back. Caphy jumped to her feet and shot toward the front door. "Incoming!" I warned.

A beat later, I heard Lis squeal and laugh as she no doubt found herself wrangling an eighty-pound pibl. "Jeeze!" she complained, coming into the kitchen. "That dog's a menace."

Despite her declaration, my friend was sans pitty. "Where'd she go?"

"I opened the door, and she did a drive-by licking on her way to the front yard." She showed me the large wet spot on her knee.

"Coffee?"

Lis shook her head. "I need to meet a client up the street for a showing in fifteen minutes. I just thought I'd stop in and see how you're doing." She gave me a sly look that told me exactly why she was really there.

"You mean you want to know what's going on with the murder investigation?"

She dropped onto the stool next to me. "Well, if you insist on talking about it."

I laughed. "The victim is the caterer. All we've learned so far is that Cecily might have threatened him earlier in the day, and the dessert guy clearly knows something he's not letting on."

She gave me exaggerated wide eyes. "Not the dessert guy!"

"I know, right?"

"Protect him at all costs. Those tiny key lime pie things were to die for."

I snorted. "Seriously though, do you remember how Cecily reacted when we found the victim? I've been trying to remember, but I was kind of distracted."

Lis grimaced. "I was kind of distracted by the dead guy too. And the shrieking."

I nodded. "That server's name is Karinne Magness. She's the one who told me that Cecily threatened Jonathan Calliente."

"Karinne Magness?"

I nodded, noting the surprise on Lis's face. "You know her?"

Instead of answering, she reached over and took my coffee, sipping from it and then grimacing. "How much sugar did you put in this?"

I reclaimed my mug. "The perfect amount for me. Get your own."

She did as I suggested, sliding a dark roast pod into the single-serving brewer. "I met Karinne a couple of months ago. She and her husband...Mark, I think...looked at a couple of houses in the new developments."

Deer Hollow had somehow been highlighted as one of

the best places to live and raise a family a couple of years earlier. Ever since that article, we'd been the unwilling victims of an influx of people from Indianapolis and surrounding cities whose crime and cost of living made them less desirable places to live. One of the consequences of that influx had been two new subdivisions. The other was too much traffic and an overburdening of our simple, outdated resources.

But one person's bane was another's boon. Deer Hollow Realty was definitely benefiting from all those new homes.

"Did they buy?" I asked.

Lis leaned against the counter with her black coffee, sipping carefully. "No. I think they decided to move to the outskirts of Indy. If I remember right, her mom lived there, and she wanted to stay close."

I could certainly understand that. "What was she like?"

Lis frowned. "The mom?"

"No." I laughed. "Karinne. I can't decide what I think of her. She seems okay, but there's just something..."

"Off about her?" Lis finished for me, nodding. "I agree. I also got the impression the couple was having issues. I think, ultimately, that was what made them decide to stay close to family."

"Was she working at the catering company then?"

"I don't think she was working. The job might be something new."

"Like something a woman getting a divorce would do?"

"Yep." Lis glanced at her watch. "Ah! I need to go. Keep me updated on things, will you? I feel like I have a stake in this, given that I was there when the victim was discovered." She arched an eyebrow. "You understand that feeling, right?"

Since I'd lost count of the number of bodies I'd nearly stumbled over, I certainly did.

My phone rang as Lis left. It was Hal. "Hey," I said, smiling in spite of myself.

"Hey, honey. How'd you sleep?"

"I would have slept great if I wasn't clinging to the edge of the bed without any covers."

"Caphy?"

"And her evil feline sidekick. I swear LaLee takes up more room than the eighty-pound dog."

His chuckle made my stomach do a happy dance. "Do you feel like visiting Cecily this morning? I want to catch her at home. Tomorrow, she'll be back in the office, and it'll be harder to get her alone."

"I can be ready in twenty minutes."

CECILY ADDAMS LIVED in a tidy clapboard home in the woods, not too far from Benson Dexter, the man who'd tried to take Mayor Robb's job away from him and failed in a spectacular way. He was also Cecily's boyfriend, a fact that put her in an extremely tenuous situation. If her boss found out who she was seeing in her spare time, she'd be out of a job pretty quickly.

I couldn't help but wonder if any of that had something to do with Cecily threatening Calliente.

The craftsman-style home was small but charming, with scalloped siding, a central peak, and a porch with wide pillars that ran the length of the house. The porch held several large clay pots filled with flowers and two comfy-looking rockers.

I looked out over the property as Hal rang the bell, marveling at the tidiness of the flower beds and yard. Cecily Addams either spent a lot of money hiring out the upkeep for her yard, or she spent most of her free time doing it herself.

The door opened after the second ring. Cecily stood on the other side of a screen door, a dishtowel in her hands and her blonde hair in a messy twist that allowed almost more hair to escape than she had trapped.

Drying her hands on the towel, she smiled at us. "What a nice surprise. Did you learn something about the murder at Mayor Robb's party?"

She certainly didn't act like she had anything to hide. But if Karinne had been telling the truth, Cecily had to know that threatening someone mere minutes before he's found dead is bound to earn her a few extra questions from the police, at the very least.

"Your home is beautiful," I said, in lieu of answering her question.

"Thank you. Come in out of the heat. It's going to be close to ninety today." She grimaced, clearly not a fan of the heat.

We followed her into a living room that was a fun mix of shabby chic and country modern.

"Sit. Would you like something cold to drink?" She shoved hair off her moist face. "I'm going to have something. I just came in from working in the yard. I try to get my work done early, before the heat sets in. But I didn't quite make it today."

Well, that answered that.

"I have lemonade."

"That sounds wonderful," I told her.

The kitchen was separated from the living room by a wide archway. She spoke to us as she assembled three glasses of lemonade. "I've been thinking about Calliente's death. I remember Mayor Robb went into the house for a few minutes. I wonder if he could have seen something?"

Or killed the man himself, I thought.

Hal walked along a wall of built-ins, reading the titles on Cecily's collection of hardcover books. "He insists he never went further than the laundry room," my PI said.

I took the frosty glass Cecily handed me. "Thank you. This looks delicious." She'd included a twist of mint and a slice of lemon on the rim, which was covered in sugar.

I tasted it and nearly swooned with pleasure. The sweet iciness was perfect for cooling down on a hot day. "That's amazing."

Cecily smiled. "I'm glad you like it. I'm kind of serious about my lemonade." Leaving the room again, she returned with two more tall glasses, handing one to Hal. She took a seat in an old-fashioned wooden rocker with tie-on cushions. Like everything else in the home, it was pretty and comfortable. It was clear Cecily Addams liked nice things. But she seemed to put an equal amount of stock into comfort.

She looked up at Hal, who hadn't taken a seat yet. "Please," she said, giving him a smile. "Sit. I'll get a crick in my neck talking to you."

"Sorry." He sat. "I was just admiring your book collection. You have a lot of the classics."

Her face lit up. "I do. I love them. Today's works are just so rushed compared to the classics. People knew how to take their time with a story years ago."

"In all fairness," I said. "In those days, readers wanted to take their time with a story too. With today's hurry up so you can rush faster mentality, I'm not sure Jane Austin would be nearly as popular."

Cecily laughed. "You make a good point." She eyed Hal.

"Obviously, you came to talk to me about something. Why don't you just tell me what it is."

Straightforward and seemingly without guilt. I was having trouble picturing Cecily as our murderer. But then, if she were the murderer, that would be exactly the impression she'd want to give.

6

"We have a witness who heard you threatening the victim before he was killed. We wanted to get your side of the story."

Cecily paled, clearly surprised. "Witness?"

It was interesting that was the part she'd glommed onto from Hal's statement.

"Who was it?"

Hal shook his head. "I can't give you information about an ongoing investigation." He smiled to soften his words. "Can you speak to the charge?"

Cecily stared at him a long moment, the sweat from her glass dripping onto the plush, cream and rose rug beneath our feet. Finally, she bowed her head. "Your witness is right. I did threaten Jonathan."

"About what?" Hal asked.

"He was skimming money, overcharging the mayor's office for the catering services. I told him either he needed to give me a corrected bill, or I'd make sure he never worked another catering job in this area again."

"How'd you know he was skimming?" I asked.

She glanced quickly my way. "I have a source on his staff. Someone very reliable."

Hal and I both stared at her, and she sighed. "I used to date him. We parted amicably and have remained friends."

I had a suspicion who the friendly ex might be. "Prince?"

She twitched in surprise. "How'd you know?"

"We met him and Karinne last night. At Sonny's Diner," Hal said.

Cecily frowned. "Karinne?"

"The screamer from the crime scene," I told her, raising my brows.

"Oh." Cecily gave me a small smile. "That server woman. I didn't know she was seeing Prince."

Her question was probably meant to sound like a throwaway. A simple observation. But I heard the note of curiosity in it. "I don't know if they're seeing each other or not," I said, shrugging.

When she realized I wasn't going to expound on that, she nodded. "I didn't take him at his word, of course. I'm not in the business of flinging careless accusations around. I contacted one of Calliente Catering's references and encouraged her to be honest. The client I spoke to denied he'd overcharged her. But she did finally admit she'd heard rumblings from unsatisfied clients. Two of those clients were happy to speak to me about the company."

"Do you think his bad business practices got him killed?" Hal asked Cecily.

"If you're asking me whether the two clients I spoke to were mad enough to kill him, the answer is, probably not. They were understandably peeved about it. One of them reported him to the Better Business Bureau and the

Attorney General's office. But nothing came of either attempt to seek justice. They were mad and frustrated, but the amount of money he skimmed from them was only a few thousand in each case. Not enough to risk prison time over."

"How about his employees?" I asked. "How does...did... he treat them?"

Cecily shifted in her chair, looking uncomfortable. "He treated them fine, as far as I can tell. Prince didn't mention any mistreatment. Not from Jonathan."

My brows rose at that little qualification. "But they were mistreated by someone else in the company?"

"What I'm going to tell you is a rumor, pure and simple. Please don't treat it as anything more than that."

Hal nodded.

"Jonathan has a fiancée. Pammie. I don't know her last name. She runs the office and oversees the servers during events. Prince hates her, and apparently he isn't alone."

I didn't remember seeing a woman running around managing the servers, and I told her as much.

"That's because she was gone by the time you arrived. I spoke briefly to her before the party. But at some point, she disappeared. I was looking for her right before the party started and nobody had seen her for several minutes. I never did see her after that."

Hal and I shared a look. The fiancée's disappearance was a giant red flag. Had she killed Calliente and then bolted?

"You say she ran the office. Is it possible she was the one overcharging clients?"

"I couldn't say. It seems plausible." Cecily smiled. "Bridezilla tendencies are their own special kind of madness."

HAL CHECKED in with Arno on our way to speak to the server known as Prince. "Arno, you have Joey and me. We just spoke to Cecily Addams."

"The mayor's assistant? Did you learn anything useful?"

Hal quickly filled him in on our conversation with Cecily. "We're heading over to the Deer Hollow Motel to speak with Prince the dessert guy now."

"Good. We've hit kind of a dead-end here. We only found one partial fingerprint on the knife block, and it's not enough for an ID."

"Nothing on the knife?" Hal asked.

"Wiped clean. The counter and block also appear to have been wiped. The partial we found was underneath the lip of the counter."

"The killer wouldn't have had much time to wipe the place down. Maybe he missed something else."

"Yeah. I'm sending Deputy Sheppard out to have another look today. Maybe we'll get lucky. Let's touch base at the end of the day, and we can compare notes."

Hal turned into the parking lot of the Deer Hollow Motel and parked in front of the office. "Talk to you then." Disconnecting, he glanced at me. "I'll talk to the manager. Do you want to wait here?"

I nodded, "I need to make a phone call."

Watching Hal stride toward the end unit with a sign over the door announcing it as the office, I dialed Lis. She answered three rings later, sounding breathless. "Hey, girlfriend."

"Hey. How'd your showing go?"

"Great. I just wrote up an offer. Cross your fingers for me that the seller takes it."

"All my digits are crossed. It's going to be hard to use my hands and feet, though."

She chuckled. "You can uncross. It's the spirit of the thing that counts."

"Whew!" I said, grinning.

"You need help with something?"

"I do." I hesitated, knowing that what I was about to ask her for would probably be a breach of her realtor's code. "We might need to talk to Karinne's husband."

After dropping that bomb, I just let it sit there between us like a bad odor. I could almost visualize Lis wrinkling her nose. Finally, she said. "Can you ask Karinne to give you his number?"

"I can. And, I will. But if she won't share..."

"Then I need the request to come from the police."

"Will Hal do? He's working with the sheriff's office."

She sighed. "I can make that work. But try not to have to ask me, okay?"

"I promise. Here comes Hal. I'll talk to you later?"

"You'd better. I want to know how our investigation is coming along."

I grinned. "*Our* investigation?"

"Bye, Joe."

I joined my PI on the sidewalk.

"He's in unit eight."

Hal knocked on the door to number eight and I glanced around, noting the lack of cars and the unkempt feeling of the place. "They're not exactly flush with business here."

Hal knocked again. "I think your future stepdad's new hotel is hurting them." He grinned. "People inexplicably opt for clean rooms and stunning views over unidentifiable stains and cockroaches."

"Imagine that," I said, grimacing.

Nobody answered the door, but I heard a muffled thump from inside the room.

Hal frowned. "Did you hear that?"

I nodded.

Hal peered through the large window beside the door. The drapes were closed, but they gaped in the middle. He suddenly moved away from the window and positioned himself in front of the door. "Stand back!"

I got out of his way and he slammed a foot into the door, right next to the knob. The flimsy door splintered and slammed inward, crashing loudly against something behind it.

Hal was inside the room and running before I could even step through.

I found him hanging out an open window on the back wall. "Prince is running?" I asked, not believing it.

Hal pulled back inside, shaking his head. "No." He nodded toward something on the floor between two full-sized beds. It took my brain a minute to register that it was Prince. "Whoever did *that* is running."

I stepped toward Prince, but Hal eased past me. "Don't touch anything. Can you call an ambulance?"

I nodded and stepped out of the room, calling 9-1-1. As I dialed, a small, white car came around the end of the building and hit the gas, squealing past me and barely slowing as it left the lot and barreled into traffic. The irate blaring of horns followed the car's wild dash down the street.

"Idiot," I said, shaking my head.

Hal came out a minute later. "He's alive, though he's got a pretty good graze on his head. The bullet is embedded in the wall over the nightstand."

"What is going on?" I asked my PI.

He rubbed his forehead, looking perplexed. "I don't know. But I think it's safe to say the murder at Robb's house wasn't a simple crime of passion."

7

Arno was standing in front of the big window behind his desk, staring out at the traffic speeding down the highway. He turned when we came inside. He'd been expecting us. Motioning to the two black leather chairs on the other side of his desk, he dropped into his own seat. "The plot thickens, huh?" He smiled, but the curve of his lips seemed pasted onto his weary face. It didn't reach his eyes.

"How is he?" Hal asked. "I called the hospital, but they wouldn't tell me anything."

"He'll have a heck of a headache and he's expected to be unconscious for a while, but the docs expect him to live." Arno leaned back in his chair. "You two probably saved his life. The assailant missed the first time, but he probably would have finished the job if you hadn't shown up." He frowned. "You're sure you didn't see anything?"

Hal shook his head. "Whoever it was slipped out the window in the back. There were no footprints I could follow and there are woods behind the motel. He must have ducked into the trees."

"We ran plates on the cars in the lot, and they're all accounted for. Whoever the shooter was, he or she didn't park a car there."

"That would have been too easy," I grumbled. I thought of the small car speeding from the lot and gave myself a mental kick. "Actually, he might have. I didn't make the connection at the time, but when I was calling 9-1-1, a car sped around the building and shot into the street. I just thought it was some punk being obnoxious. But now that I think about it, he wasn't exactly driving a muscle car. There was no reason to act like a street racer."

Arno perked up, leaning forward and grabbing a pad and pen. "What did it look like?"

I described the white car as best I could remember, even coming up with an additional detail. "There was a sticker on the back bumper. It was half torn off, but there was a silver swirl, and I could just make out the word *Success*. That's all I remember."

Frowning slightly, Arno asked, "Did you get a look at the driver? License plate?"

"The car was going so fast, my brain didn't have time to register too many details. I'm sorry."

"This will help," Arno said. "At the very least, if we get a suspect, we can see if he drives a similar vehicle.

"What do we know about this Prince guy?" Hal asked the cop.

"Not much. He has no record. Not even a speeding ticket in the system. He appears to be squeaky clean."

"Is Prince his legal name?"

"Part of it," Arno said. "Anthony Prince is thirty-six, lives in Bloomington, and has only worked for Calliente Catering for three months. He appears to be a hard worker. He's worked his way up from serving non-alcoholic drinks to desserts in the short time he's been there. Some of the other servers consider him a bit of a brown nose. He has apparently spent a lot of time sucking up to the owner."

"That doesn't sound like a guy somebody would want to take a shot at."

"No," Arno agreed on a frown. "It doesn't. We didn't find any sign of drugs or even alcohol in the room where he was staying."

I thought about what I'd seen in the room the short time I'd been there. "He's actually staying at the motel? I didn't see any suitcases. And Bloomington is only half an hour away. Why wouldn't he just go home?"

"There were clothes in the bathroom," Hal said. "And toiletries. He was set to stay for a night or two at least."

"You saw him at Sonny's Diner with one of the other servers, right?" Arno asked.

"Karinne. I can't remember what she told me her last name was. She was the witness you spoke to at the scene."

"Karinne Magness. Did the two of them look like they were dating?"

I wasn't sure. "If they were, the relationship was new enough that they were still awkward around each other."

"Any idea what they were doing together?"

"Maybe they just wanted company for dinner. If they're both here from out of town, that would make sense," Hal offered.

Arno nodded. "I'll look into both of their backgrounds again. I have a feeling they're connected somehow. But on the surface, I'm not seeing it." He glanced at Hal. "Would you mind talking to Calliente's fiancée? I'm still mopping up the party people."

"Absolutely."

JONATHAN CALLIENTE'S FIANCÉE, Pammie, was staying at the Fawn Hotel outside of town. As would be expected by the name, it was built alongside the Fawn River and boasted the fact that every room had a large window and balcony overlooking the churning waters of the Fawn.

The hotel had recently changed hands and been completely renovated by the man my mother was in love with. Judging by the number of cars in the lot, Garland Medford had another successful business on his hands.

Pammie, whose last name we'd learned was Wickham, was staying in the last unit on the top floor. The room had two walls of windows overlooking the river, rather than just one, and was the Fawn's most expensive unit.

Hal knocked twice before we heard footsteps approaching the door.

Calliente's fiancée looked to be Asian Indian, with warm brown skin, thick black hair that fell several inches below her shoulders, and a slim, elegant build. Her dark eyes flashed when she saw Hal, interest clear in their depths. The soft curve of her cherry-red lips made sure he didn't miss the invitation in her gaze. "Hello." She reached a long-fingered hand toward him and he clasped it in a brisk shake.

"Ms. Wickham, my name is Hal Amity. I'm working with the sheriff's department on the investigation into your fiancé's death."

Giving him an insincere moue of sadness, she held onto my PI's hand as he gently tried to disengage. Short of wrenching it free, Hal couldn't extricate himself from her hungry clutches.

I stuck my hand into the mix, forcing her to reluctantly

drop Hal's and take it. "Joey Fulle. I'm with him." Okay, my tone might have been a bit territorial. Maybe even hostile. But I felt an instinctual need to stake my claim in the face of the other woman's rampant aggression.

Pammie curled her lips at me, an expression that was more snarl than smile. "You don't look like a policewoman."

Before I could respond, Hal said, "Can we come inside? We'd like to talk to you about Jonathan."

His reminder that she had a dead fiancé should have shamed the other woman, but she actually looped her arm through Hal's and tugged him inside.

I followed along, trying not to growl.

"Can I get you a drink?" Pammie asked Hal.

I almost said I'd like one, just to force her to notice my presence in the room. But I bit back the words, knowing her unwanted attention was nothing Hal hadn't dealt with before. He could handle it. So, I sat on the couch next to Hal and earned myself a glower when she realized that relegated her to the chair across from him.

Giving the room a quick once-over, I admired the stunning view and the classy furnishings. I could see my mother's hand in the way the room was pulled together.

"Ms. Wickham," Hal started.

"Call me Pammie, please," she gushed.

I noticed her accent, which had been very slight when she met us at the door, had grown thicker.

He gave her a mirthless smile. "First of all, I'm so sorry for your loss."

She winced slightly, clearly catching what my PI was throwing down. If she wasn't actually mourning for poor Jonathan, she should at least act as if she was. "It's just horrible."

I watched with awe as she managed to wrench out a

couple of tears. "We had such wonderful plans for Calliente Catering."

I heard two key things in that statement. One, the most important takeaway for her, apparently, was the business. And second, she spoke of him without bobbling the tense thing. Most people who lose loved ones continue to speak of them as if they were alive at first. By contrast, killers sometimes found it easy to put their victims into the past.

"You were active in the business?" Hal asked, carefully clueless.

"Oh yes," she gave him a bright smile. "We were partners in every sense. I have a master's in business, you know. I have plans to turn the company into a national success."

Hal's midnight brows lifted. "You're going to expand throughout the country?"

"I am."

Hal's lips twitched slightly. Pammie didn't realize the trap he'd led her into. "So, with Mr. Calliente's death, you inherit the business?"

She blinked slowly, like a reptile, and her lips flapped a few times while she made several false starts on a response. She'd just realized how nakedly ambitious she'd sounded. "I've put my heart and soul into the business. But I'm not glad he's dead if that's what you're implying."

Hal's smile was brilliant. "I'm not implying anything, Pammie. I'm just trying to discover who killed Jonathan."

She nodded, looking a little green around the gills.

"Do you have any idea who might have wanted him dead?" Hal asked. "A competitor? An angry customer? A scorned lover?"

Pammie bristled at the last suggestion. "Jonathan wasn't cheating on me."

I let my eyes go wide. "Are you sure? You said yourself

that you were working very hard building the company. Maybe he felt neglected."

Her lips curled again. There might have been a growl.

I chewed my lip to keep from smiling.

She shook her head, then smoothed the glossy perfection of her hair. "Jonathan was a dreamer. He had a lot of ideas, but he could never settle down enough to see any of them through. He was our concept person. I took care of the day-to-day details. Everybody knew that. If a client was going to take something out on someone, it would have probably been me."

"Were there angry clients who might have been looking for payback?"

She shrugged. "People want the world, but when it comes down to it, they often don't want to pay for it. I'm used to that."

"Have you been threatened?" Hal asked.

Her gaze slid sideways, telling me she had. "I have thick skin and ironclad contracts. I don't worry about that type of thing."

"Humor me," Hal said. "Who might have wanted Jonathan dead?"

She thought about it for a beat and then said, "If you're looking for someone who was angry at Johnny, you don't have to look far. Mayor Robb was here night before last, screaming at the top of his lungs."

"What about?" I asked before I could stop myself.

Pammie threw me a snarl and then pointed her response to Hal instead. "He accused Johnnie of telling secrets to his enemies."

"What secrets?" Hal asked.

She shrugged again. "I don't know. But I didn't get the

impression that they were talking about catering. You know what I mean?"

8

"It's time to talk to Cecily again," Hal said.

I tensed, not liking that idea at all. But I knew it had to be done. "Can we eat first? I'm starving."

He gave me a smile. "Of course. Where would you like to go?"

"Home? We still have our dinners from helping Max."

"And pie," he said, waggling his brows.

He knew me so well. "And pie," I agreed with a laugh.

Caphy was flinging herself at the door as we parked Hal's SUV in the turnaround in front of the house. The pibl punctuated each of her body slams against my long-suffering door with unhappy sounds that were half howling and half yodeling.

The couple sitting in the swing on the porch kept sliding worried looks toward the sound. They were probably wondering why I had a yodeling wolf living in my house.

I waved at Cecily and her boyfriend, Benson Dexter, as I climbed the steps. "Hey, you two. Did I forget a visit?"

Cecily wrapped me in a hug. "No. We took a chance and stopped by."

"I hope you haven't been waiting long."

Benson hugged me too and shook Hal's hand. "Only a few minutes. And we've been serenaded the entire time." He threw a pointed look toward the door, which had been abandoned. Hearing our voices, Caphy had relocated to the living room window and was yodeling there instead.

"We were just going to have some lunch. Would you like to join us?"

"We don't want to intrude," Cecily said, though I got the sense she wanted to stay.

"Come on," I urged, sliding my arm through hers. "Max sent us home with two massive portions of chicken and noodles last night. And a whole pie."

Her eyes lit. "Banana cream pie?"

"Is there any other kind?"

At the door, I hesitated, glancing at Hal. "You'd better work your magic, or she's going to flatten everybody."

He unlocked the door and opened it just wide enough that he could still block it with his body. "Beauty, sit."

I watched my crazy dog drop ungracefully to her fuzzy butt and stare up at him with an adoring gaze.

He held up a hand, palm out and said, "Stay."

Her tail skimmed the tile of the entry and her beautiful green eyes swung to Cecily and Benson, but she didn't jump up.

Hal turned his hand over and wiggled his fingers, pulling a treat from his pocket and saying, "Easy, girl."

Caphy took the treat, swallowed it without chewing, and walked over to give Cecily's knee a lick. She picked up a little speed as she swiped her tongue over the knee of Benson's jeans and then took off running to do her business.

Hal laughed. "It's not foolproof. There's only so much you can do with that much enthusiasm."

"I'd forgotten how gorgeous she is," Benson said. He glanced at Hal. "By the way, I wanted to thank you for telling me about the rescue fundraiser." He and Cecily shared a look. "We each rescued a senior dog. We're in love."

"I took a cat too," Cecily said, chuckling. "I didn't realize how much I missed having a pet until I brought those two into my house. You should see the antics they get up to."

"I believe it," I told her. "Caphy and LaLee are in a constant state of hijinks." I frowned. "I'm surprised we didn't see your furbabies when we visited."

Cecily nodded. "The pup was sleeping in her favorite sunbeam in my bedroom. She's kind of hard of hearing, so she probably didn't hear you arrive. The cat was likely asleep too." She laughed. "They're very low-key, which is good. I couldn't imagine going from no pet to a pet that bounced off the walls."

Right on cue, an elongated squeal preceded the burst of a black and white projectile wearing a purple sparkly t-shirt through the door. Our miniature pot-bellied pig, Ethel Squeaks, toddled over to us. Her tail twirling, she bumped first me and then Hal in the thigh with her twitching snout.

"She's hungry," I explained. "Let's go inside and feed her before she kneecaps us."

As we walked through the house, Cecily ogled Ethel. "That t-shirt is adorable."

I nodded. "It was a gift from her aunt Lis." The shirt said *Princess Porkpie* on the back in pink sequins. "I don't know where Lis finds them, but Ethel has a better wardrobe than I do."

Cecily laughed with delight.

Hal came into the kitchen sans Benson. At Cecily's questioning look, he said, "Men's room."

"Ah." She sat on a stool at the counter and watched me

put together a plate full of fruit and raw veggies. Ethel trotted around my feet, bumping me energetically as she continued to make soft snorting noises. "She hasn't eaten in a couple of hours. She thinks she's dying," I explained.

Laughing, Cecily said, "I know how she feels."

I placed the plate on the floor by Ethel's tent, and she dove in. Picking up Caphy's bowl, I put assorted melon chunks and strawberries into it. As if she could smell her snack, the pitty barreled into the room and skidded to a halt mere inches from where I placed her bowl. "She has to eat whenever Ethel eats. Thank goodness she loves fruit and veggies too, or she'd be as fat as a house by now."

"She'll eat veggies?" Cecily asked, shocked.

"Raw carrots and broccoli mostly. But she loves every kind of fruit."

"No grapes, though," Hal said. "They're poisonous to dogs."

"I did not know that," Cecily said. "That's good to know. I love grapes. I'll have to be careful. Anything else?"

"Raisins, chocolate, I wouldn't give him? Her?"

"Her. I named her Mandy."

"I love that name," I said.

"She just looked like a Mandy to me. My cat's name is Divet. He's black and gray with white stripes. A gorgeous boy."

"Divet?" Hal asked. "That's unique."

Nodding, Cecily said, "It was the name he came with. Since he's a cat, I figured he wouldn't humor me by taking a new name. He barely answers to the one he has."

Hal placed four plates on the counter, and we divvied up the dinners from Sonny's Diner.

"Anyway, I wouldn't give her raw potato either. I'm pretty sure they're toxic to dogs," I said.

"Good to know." She eyed the food as if she hadn't eaten in days.

She caught me watching her and laughed. "I was too upset to eat last night. And this morning, I didn't have time."

Hal put a plate into the microwave and covered it. "After eating this, you won't need to eat until tomorrow."

Cecily and I shared a look, and she blew a raspberry. "Spoken like a man."

I nodded, patting him on the back. "Eating has nothing to do with need and everything to do with *need*."

"Truth," Cecily agreed.

We carried our plates and glasses of frosty lemonade to the back porch and sat under a ceiling fan out of the sun to eat. Caphy sat with her head in my lap but mostly didn't beg.

Ethel wandered around the yard, snorfling around the base of the trees in search of succulent roots.

We made small talk as we ate, the late afternoon sun painting the grass and trees of my backyard in shades of gold. As we reached the bottom of our plates, we sat back with full bellies and enjoyed watching the animals play for a few moments.

Finally, Benson sat forward, a serious expression on his face. "I'm sure you're wondering why we're here."

"I think I have a pretty good idea," Hal said. "You came to explain why Cecily threatened Jonathan Calliente right before he died."

Cecily flinched, setting down her fork. "I know that looks bad." She looked at me. "I'm sorry I didn't come clean about it. The thing is, I knew it would make me a suspect."

"And now?" I asked, trying to keep my tone neutral.

"Now, I realize it was stupid to think I could hide it. I

know Karinne heard me. Deputy Willager has already asked me about it."

"Did you tell him the truth?" Hal asked.

She flinched again. The woman would be toast at the poker table. "What I told him was the truth."

"But not all of the truth," Hal guessed.

"No." She sighed. "Not all of it."

"You realize that even lying by omission just makes you look guiltier," he said softly.

She nodded. "I do. That's why we're here."

"She was trying to protect me," Benson said into the silence that followed.

"Why would she need to protect you?" Hal asked.

Benson sighed. "I hired Calliente Catering for a party last week. I knew Robb used them, and to be honest, I'd heard the owners had flexible values."

"What do you mean by that?" I asked.

Benson flicked me a guilty look. "The word on Calliente and his partner is that they'll do just about anything for money. I might have taken advantage of that impulse."

"How so?" Hal asked.

Benson and Cecily shared a look. She gave him the slightest of nods. He reluctantly went on. "I...bribed... Jonathan Calliente to do a little snooping for me while at Robb's home."

"Snooping for what?" Hal asked.

Benson shook his head, staring at his hands.

"Evidence of Robb molesting a young intern early in his political career," Cecily replied when he wouldn't.

I stared blankly at her, not believing what I was hearing. "That happened?"

Cecily nodded. "Robb and his powerful friends have done a nice job of covering it up. The girl was paid off, and her identity was kept away from everybody. The only ones who know are Robb and the high-level cop in Indianapolis he paid off to keep it secret. But there was definitely a girl."

"How do you know about it?" Hal asked, his expression clearly showing his disgust.

Benson sighed. "I worked as an intern in his office back then."

"Then you know the identity of the girl."

Benson shook his head. "I was new and Robb had me out doing grunt work, handing out fliers and stuff. But when I came back to the office late one night, I overheard a couple of women talking about it. I guess the girl he molested left that day. The speculation was that she was paid off. I couldn't get anybody in the office to talk to me about it because they were afraid they'd get fired. Or worse."

"I don't understand," I said. "This would have been..."

"Fifteen years ago," Benson said.

"Why do you think you'd find anything now? That was a long time ago." I said.

Benson looked at Cecily.

She clasped his hand. "Robb keeps things to use against people. It's one of the reasons he's gotten where he is. The man has aspirations to run for governor and, from there, the presidency. He knows there will be people who try to get in his way, so he does what he needs to do to make sure that doesn't happen."

"Like when he framed me," Benson said.

Robb had paid someone to drop stolen jewelry into Benson's car when Benson was running against him for mayor of Deer Hollow. His dirty trick had ultimately gotten someone killed. But he'd managed to slither his way out of it.

"He hoards knowledge," Cecily went on. "Souvenirs, blackmail items."

"So you think he's got something in his office that might incriminate him on being inappropriate with this girl?"

"And others," Cecily said, nodding. "I'd bet money on it."

"How old was the girl?" Hal asked. His jaw was tight, his lips pressed into a taut line. He was really unhappy with what Benson and Cecily were telling us.

"I don't know. I was twenty-five, but I was one of the oldest interns. Most of them were in their late teens. Some in their early twenties."

I could tell what Hal was thinking. The molestation was bad, but lots of politicians abuse their staff and get away with it. However, if the girl had been underage, even speculation of the crime might be enough to sink him.

"Does that really matter?" Cecily asked, slightly indignant. "Even if she's an adult, what he did was wrong."

"If it's true, it would be wrong," Hal agreed, speaking carefully. "But the public's reaction would be different if the girl was underage. It would be harsher, less forgiving. Which means Robb would be more desperate to keep that from being known."

I was watching Benson. He looked nervous. Almost scared. An over-the-top reaction to what they were telling us. "Why come forward with this now?" I asked.

He looked surprised. "Because you were bound to find out that Cecily fought with Calliente. I didn't want you to think she killed him."

"You could have waited to see if we suspected her," I suggested. I couldn't explain it, but I knew there was more they weren't telling us.

He sighed. "You're right. Someone is threatening me. Someone knows I paid Calliente to snoop." He looked up finally, his expression taut with worry. "I'll be honest. I'm scared. Robb's a skunk. He has friends in high and low places. If he decides he wants me dead..." Benson shook his head.

He didn't need to finish that thought. We'd all witnessed what Robb was capable of.

"Tell us what you were fighting with Calliente about," Hal asked Cecily.

She took a deep breath and expelled it slowly. "He claimed he'd found evidence, but he wanted more money for it. I told him we didn't respond well to blackmail, but he wouldn't budge." Cecily's face flushed deep red with remembered anger. "He demanded double what we'd agreed on. Or, he said he was going to tell Robb what I was doing."

She looked away, her face tight. "I know that gives me motive to kill him. But I promise I didn't do it. I was going to tell Benson to pay him what he wanted. It was the only thing we could do."

"If you didn't kill him," Hal said. "Who did?"

The pair exchanged another look. Finally, Cecily said. "Mayor Robb came into the house to make a phone call. I think he caught Calliente going through his stuff. I think he killed him and then returned to his party, cool as you please."

I was very afraid she was right. I was also afraid that was bad news. Because, in all likelihood, it meant the killer would get away with murder.

"Pam Wickham is the obvious prospect to be the blackmailer," Hal said.

We were once again sitting on the back porch, and I was watching him grill burgers for our dinner. We'd spent the day researching and calling Calliente Catering clients from a list Benson had given us. As expected, the largest percentage of them felt as if they'd been over-charged, and a couple of them were potential blackmail victims. But we couldn't get them to open up to us over the phone.

Hal scooped two small patties off the grill and placed them on a platter to cool. The tiny burgers were for Caphy and Ethel Squeaks. I'd give LaLee some of mine. I could definitely eat an entire burger myself, but I was trying not to. As I got closer to thirty, all the pie and carbs I'd been eating were starting to accumulate around my hips. If I was honest, the real reason I was going to cut calories with my sandwich was that I fully intended to suggest we go for ice cream after dinner. I smiled at the thought.

"Did you believe their story?" Hal asked, sliding the last two burgers onto buns.

I tossed the salad and added a dollop more Italian dressing to it, the scent of herbs and vinegar making my mouth water.

"Cecily and Benson?" I asked, shrugging. "I want to. But it works in their favor to point us in a different direction. Both had motive. In Benson's case, it's more than one motive. And Cecily had opportunity too."

I'd been ambivalent about Benson Dexter since the first time I'd met him. He was a politician. In my mind, that made everything he said suspect. But he also seemed like a decent guy. He was good to Cecily, and he loved animals. And, while his adopting a senior dog from the local shelter in a town where he's trying to get elected made my cynical side itch, I did believe he liked dogs.

"The things they told us could be possible. It's all feasible. Especially the part about Pam Wickham being a viper." My brain rebelled against calling the woman "Pammie." She was a grown woman, and the moniker made her sound five.

Hal put the platter on the table between us, and I cut one of the small burgers into tiny pieces. I added some salad to the top and put it on the floor in front of Ethel. Hal fixed Caphy's plate, sans everything except carrots and cucumbers from the salad. The pitty didn't eat salad.

"Something doesn't add up," Hal said after swallowing a bite of burger. "I can't put my finger on it."

I stabbed some salad. "What do you think about the possibility that Mayor Robb killed Calliente?"

Hal wiped his mouth and sat back. "You know how much I'd like to believe he was the killer."

I nodded. "Me too."

"He had opportunity, though the timeframe was slim. If

what they said was true, he had motive. But the optics of another murder in his vicinity are really bad. This will stretch the goodwill of the police and the public."

I knew he was right but, of the suspects we had, I'd much rather believe Robb was our killer than almost anybody.

Except maybe Pam Wickham.

My phone rang, and I grinned at the ID, punching the button to answer it. "Mom! Are you and Garland back in town?" My mom and her long-time boyfriend, who she'd only recently gotten back together with, had gone to Paris and Venice for the summer. Just because.

"Hi honey! I've missed your sweet face. No, we're sitting at a little café in Paris eating croissant." She sighed. "It's so romantic here, honey. You and Hal really ought to come."

"Hi, Joey!" Garland said in the background.

"Tell him I said hi," I answered with a smile.

I ignored her suggestion, not even tempted. Even if I had a desire to travel, which I didn't, I couldn't leave my menagerie with just anybody. I'd worry about them the whole time, and it wouldn't even be fun.

But she'd think I was crazy if I told her that, so I just made agreeable noises as she told me how much fun they were having. "I'm glad you're having a good time," I said. "But I miss you guys. When are you coming back?"

"I'm not sure, honey. As soon as we figure it out, I'll let you know."

"Good."

There was a beat of silence, and I picked at my salad. There was apparently something she wanted to tell me but wasn't sure how. Finally, she said, "How's it going there? Anything new?"

I bit back a bark of laughter. *You mean like a dead body at a party? Blackmail? Threats?* "Same old, same old. Hal and I are good. The kids are good. It's all good."

"Good." She must have realized how shallow the conversation had turned. She sighed. "Well, I'll let you go. I just wanted to hear your voice."

"Okay..." I hesitated. "Mom, is there something wrong?"

"No, honey. I'll talk to you soon. Love you!"

"Love you too." I ended the call and sat staring at my plate.

Hal's hand found mine and gave it a squeeze. "Problem?"

"I'm not sure."

"Then we won't worry about it until we know it's a problem. Eat your food before it gets cold. You can't have ice cream if you don't eat at least half of your dinner."

I grinned at him, the strange phone call forgotten. The man really got me. Sometimes I thought he knew me better than I knew myself.

I MOANED with heartfelt enthusiasm as I slipped the first bite of dark hot fudge over sweet, creamy vanilla ice cream into my mouth. I closed my eyes as the treat melted over my taste buds. It was almost as good as Banana cream pie.

Almost.

"That good, huh?" Hal's delectable lips curved into a genuine smile.

Not as good as that smile. "Amazing."

A long chorus of pathetic whining sifted through the open window in the car, which was parked under the shady branches of a nearby tree. The whining was accompanied by a loud squeal that made the poor woman at the order window yelp and throw her hands into the air.

I winced, watching the two cups of ice cream she'd been holding fly through the air and splat onto the sidewalk.

Her three toddlers, two boys and a tiny girl, burst into tears at the sight. Inconsolable.

Hal patted my hand. "I'll take care of it."

I watched him stride toward the frazzled mother, who was holding the little girl and trying to soothe all three of the kids. She looked up as he addressed her, and the tension streamed from her curvy form when Hal smiled. He crouched down and spoke to the two boys. Within seconds, he had them both giggling, and their mother wasn't far behind. Hal went to the window and said something to the order clerk.

A few minutes later, the kids were holding fresh ice creams and their mother looked like she'd be willing to leave her family behind and run away with my boyfriend. I fought a smile as Hal returned.

"The magic of Hal Amity," I said as he scooped a bite of half-melted ice cream into his mouth. "What did you say to them?"

He grabbed a paper napkin and dabbed his lips. "I promised they could come see Ethel Squeaks when they were done with their ice cream."

"No wonder," I said. "What self-respecting country kid doesn't want to see a pig in a tee-shirt."

"That's what I thought. We shared a grin and he leaned close, pressing his cold, sweet-tasting lips to mine. It didn't take long for our lips to heat back up."

At the sound of a gently cleared throat, we jumped guiltily apart. The woman with the kids was staring at us with a shy smile. "Is this a bad time?"

Hal untangled himself from the bench of the picnic table. "Not at all. That was fast."

The woman sighed. "I'm sorry. But once you told them about the pig, they didn't want their ice cream anymore." If she was upset about that, it didn't show in her pleasant face.

He laughed good-naturedly. "No problem. She is kind of a rock star." He squeezed my shoulder, murmuring, "I'll be back in a few."

I nodded and gave myself over to the last of my ice cream sundae. My attention was caught by the shrieks and giggling behind me, and I laughed as Ethel trotted from kid to kid and then to mom, tail spinning and happy snout twitching. Princess Piggy did love being the center of attention. But then Hal brought Caphy out, and the happy squeals reached a crescendo. The kids were smitten.

Caphy got her ice cream second-hand, licking it from the kids' hands and shirt fronts.

I'll never know what made me turn my head toward the back of the parking lot. It was shrouded in mature trees, the entire end of the lot a shady haven that usually held several cars with dogs that were waiting patiently for their ice-cream-bearing owners. A cornfield butted up against the lot, the stalks reaching well over my head and forming a perfect backdrop for the two people standing near an expensive-looking sports car.

I didn't recognize them at first, but when I did, surprise kept me rooted to the spot. "What in the world?" I was dimly aware of laughter behind me but couldn't seem to turn my gaze away from the sight of Mayor Robb and Karinne from Calliente Catering. At well over six feet tall, Robb towered over Karinne, and her body language said everything there was to say.

Karinne had folded in on herself, her slender arms wrapping her in a defensive hug. Her chin was tilted downward, her gaze on her feet, and Robb was poking a finger at her, jabbing in what could only be perceived as a threatening action. Though the mayor was slender, the ropey muscles of his arms and calves implied a strength that had probably been honed in a gym rather than built naturally through genetics.

Used to seeing him in perfectly fitted dark suits with crisp white button-down shirts and power ties, I found it odd to see him dressed in a polo shirt and khaki shorts.

Before I considered what I was doing, I was on my feet, striding toward them. When I was ten feet away from the pair, the mayor turned my way, the angry infusion of color in his cheeks flaring brighter when he spotted me.

Karinne shrank back as if considering an escape through the cornfield.

"Is there a problem?" I asked, a frown taking over my face. I didn't like bullies. And I especially didn't like when men bullied those who were smaller and weaker than they were.

"Mind your own business Fulle," Robb growled out. "This has nothing to do with you."

Ignoring him, I looked at Karinne. "Are you all right?"

The woman's eyes flashed with something that looked like anger. She raised her chin. "I'm fine. As he said, it's none of your concern."

I didn't let her attitude fool me. Fear was threaded through every line of her body. She wasn't angry with me. She was angry that I'd caught her appearing weak.

I glanced toward Robb again. "I don't care if this woman worked for you at the party. You don't have the right to abuse her."

The politician's fists tightened at his sides. But he hadn't gotten as far as he had in politics by being unaware of optics. He lifted his gaze to take in the dozen or so people watching us and made a sudden, cynical calculation. I watched him morph into a political animal right before my eyes. His posture loosened, his jaw unclenched, and his expression became almost pleasant. Except for the cold steel in his gray eyes. He inclined his head. "You're right, Ms. Fulle. I forgot myself for a minute. I'm sorry."

I scowled at him, not fooled for a minute. "It's not me you need to apologize to."

He turned to Karinne, but she was already moving toward a small orange car a few parking spots away. She climbed inside the car and shot backward, nearly clipping the pickup truck next to her. Her tires kicked up gravel as she shot toward the end of the lot and exited onto the road.

I heard footsteps on the gravel behind me. Hal's warm hand found the small of my back. "Is everything okay?"

I stared at Robb. "I'm not sure. Is everything okay, Mayor Robb?"

He chuckled. "Of course. I lost my temper, but Ms. Fulle reminded me that was inappropriate for a man in my situation."

"What were you mad about," I asked.

Robb shook his head dismissively. "Nothing you need to concern yourself with."

"Actually," Hal said, his tone firm. "We're working with Sheriff Mulhern to find a killer. Since the murder happened in your home, I assume you'll want to do everything you can to help?"

It was posed as a question, but it was really more of a challenge than a request.

Robb's jaw tightened again. For a brief moment, he looked as if he were chewing his own teeth. Then he inclined his head. "Of course. Did you have questions for me?"

I jumped in before Hal could. "Why were you brow-beating one of the Calliente Catering servers?"

Robb ran long fingers through his perfectly cut brown hair. The sunlight overhead glinted in the silver strands, which only seemed to enhance his attractiveness.

Annoyingly.

"I knew Karinne a long time ago. When I saw her on Calliente's team, I was...surprised."

"Why?" Hal asked.

"Why was I surprised?" Robb asked. He shrugged. "Because I thought she had a real knack for politics. She'd been one of my most promising interns. For her to just throw all that away to serve drinks for a catering company was...criminal."

I wasn't sure he knew what that word meant. "Did you bother to ask her why she changed professions?"

He glowered down at me. Unfortunately for him, at only five feet four inches tall, I was used to people looking down on me. I liked it when they underestimated me.

"Of course, I asked her. She didn't think it was any of my business." He looked genuinely perplexed by that.

"You still haven't explained why you were yelling at Karinne," I reminded him.

"I asked her why her boss was murdered in my home." He frowned. "Strangely, she seemed to take that personally."

"Odd," I said dryly.

"Did she have any thoughts about the murder?" Hal asked, ever the cop, even years after leaving the force.

"She implied I might have had something to do with it." Robb coughed out a laugh that had little to do with humor. "Clearly, she's lost her mind."

"Karinne told the police that she overheard your assistant yelling at her boss before he was killed," Hal said.

"Do you have any idea why Cecily would have confronted Calliente?"

Robb stared at Hal for a long moment. I didn't think he was going to answer the question. But he surprised me. "She got it into her head that the company was overcharging me for the catering." He smiled fondly. "She's very protective of me like that."

"Was the company overcharging you?" Hal asked.

"I believe it was."

"Did you ask Cecily to talk to the caterer?"

"I did not. The truth is that I hired them at the last moment. I got a new donor and wanted to show her some love." He gave me a smile filled with faux charm. "Figuratively speaking."

I remembered seeing him close-talking with a platinum blonde woman at the party. At the time, I'd assumed they were romantically involved, but she could have been the new donor. Or maybe she was both.

"Do you mind my asking who she was?" Hal asked.

"I do mind. She has nothing to do with this." With that, Robb seemed to lose interest in answering questions. "Now, if you'll excuse me. I have a tee time."

"One more question," Hal said, stopping the other man. "Do you know Calliente's fiancée? Pammie Wickham?"

Robb's handsome face creased in a frown. "Unfortunately. Horrible woman. If there was any overcharging being done, I'd place the fault for that right at her door."

"You don't think Jonathan Calliente would pad his income?"

Robb shrugged. "He might give in to her for reasons other than good business. But I'd stake my career on the probability that she was the mastermind behind it. Jonathan was a weak man, but, left to his own devices, I don't believe he would have done something like that."

We watched him climb into the expensive sports car and pull out of the lot, sending up a lot less gravel than Karinne had done.

"His impression of Calliente is a bit different from Benson and Cecily's," I said.

Hal sighed. "Yeah, I noticed that."

10

We took a chance that Pam Wickham would be in her room at the Fawn Hotel. A quick call to Arno gave us the permission we needed to speak to her again.

"Just so you know," Arno said before exiting the call. "I spoke to Pammie Wickham personally. From all evidence, she's a horrible person and has probably cheated hundreds of people out of money during the course of her involvement in the catering industry. But there's nothing to suggest she killed Calliente."

"Does she get the business if he's dead?" Hal asked.

"Nope. Calliente might have shared her avarice, but he clearly didn't trust her any further than he could chuck an oversized fruitcake. He apparently left the company to a friend from college, who started the business with him and later sold his share to Calliente with the promise that, if Calliente ever wanted out, he'd sell his share back to him. We're in the process of locating the guy now. Wickham has more reason to murder that guy than Calliente."

"Not really," I said. "A woman scorned and all that. If she found out he was cutting her out of the business, she might have killed him in a fit of passion."

"Thereby ensuring she had nothing?" I could almost hear Arno shaking his head. "I'm not buying that. Emotions aside, when it comes to ensuring their survival, I find the females of our species more pragmatic than the males."

"Lis still isn't talking to you, huh?" I asked.

His response was a sigh. "Let me know what you find out from the exorable Ms. Wickham."

"Ooh, two five-dollar words in a row," I teased. "I'm impressed."

"It seems I have nothing better to do with my personal time right now than crossword puzzles," he ground out before disconnecting.

Hal and I grinned at each other. I did feel sorry for Arno, but he'd dug his own grave with Lis. He'd just have to put in the time to claw his way out.

The hotel was quieter than the last time we'd visited. Only a few cars sat in the parking lot. We climbed the stairs to Pam Wickham's room with the sound of the Fawn River creating white noise in the background.

Hal knocked and the door opened under his fist. Throwing me a look, he pulled his gun from the beltless holster clipped to the inside waistband of his jeans and glanced at me. "Stay here," he instructed in a soft, urgent voice.

I moved to the side, so I could peer through the crack he'd left, watching him check the main room and bath. He moved toward the sliding door to the balcony, which was open about eight inches. Staying behind the drapes, he made sure the balcony was clear, then motioned me inside.

I stepped into the room, realizing that what I'd first assumed was simple messiness was more than that.

The bedside table was empty. The lamp and clock that had been on the table were crushed and broken on the floor next to the bed. The bedspread was yanked off, thrown across the room, and the top sheet seemed to be missing. A water glass lay on the carpet, a dark spot surrounding it, and a nearly empty bottle of whiskey lay next to it. The strong scent of the spilled alcohol made my stomach twist.

In the bathroom, toiletries were all over the floor, the breakable items shattered against the tile as if someone had deliberately thrown them there.

The shower curtain hung crooked, the loops holding it up on one side bent and broken.

The room had been tossed.

I heard the sliding door grinding along its track as Hal came back inside. His handsome face was grim, and he was punching numbers on his phone when I joined him. Catching his eye, I had a hunch that Pam Wickham wouldn't be needing to find a new job.

My gaze slid to the balcony, and I saw something float above the floor in an errant breeze. That was when I noticed the fabric wrapped around two of the railing balusters near the bottom.

Something was hanging from those balusters, tied there, I was pretty sure, by a rope made of bedsheets.

Hal disconnected.

"Pam Wickham?" I asked.

He nodded. "I checked for a pulse. She's dead."

"THE ME HAS PRONOUNCED IT A SUICIDE," Arno told us.

My eyes went wide. "Seriously? What about the state of the room?"

Arno kept his expression carefully neutral. "Wickham was legally intoxicated. The other people in the hotel complained about loud music and thumping noises. The speculation is that she went into a rage about Calliente's death and killed herself."

"Did anybody investigate?" Hal asked.

"The manager knocked on the door around noon, but by then it was quiet, and she just left, thinking she'd dodged a bullet. My assessment, not the manager's," Arno clarified.

"She never called the police?" I made a mental note to recommend to Garland that he get a new manager.

"She did call it in. Sheriff Mulhern himself checked it out, but he didn't notify the manager he was there, so she went to check it on her own. The sheriff said the room was quiet when he got there around eleven-forty, and a maid told him Wickham had left in her car."

My surprise must have shown in my expression.

Arno misinterpreted the shock on my face. "He does occasionally do actual police work."

I snorted out a laugh. "Right. He just happened to be passing by?"

Arno looked embarrassed. "He was…In the area."

"Why would a maid tell him the woman was gone if she wasn't?" Hal asked, his expression thoughtful.

Arno shrugged. "She probably saw someone who looked like Wickham. It's not that unusual of a mistake."

Hal and I shared a look. Then he asked, "What did the ME find as TOD?"

"Around noon."

"Nobody saw anything around that time?"

Arno narrowed his gaze on Hal. "What part of suicide are you not getting?"

"You can't tell me you believe that?" I said. Arno could be difficult and stubborn, but he wasn't stupid. Far from it.

Angry color filled his face. "Are you a trained cop, Joey?"

I frowned. I hated when he used that against me. Mostly because I knew he was right. "No. But I'm developing instincts."

I'd give him credit for not laughing at me. But I couldn't miss the twitching of his lips, so I glared at him. "That woman didn't kill herself," I declared. "I'd bet my house on it."

Hal placed a hand over mine to calm me down. "I agree with Joey. That was not a suicide."

"Based on what?" Arno asked, his tone cool.

"Based on everything else that's happened. First, Calliente is killed. Now his partner. And a third employee of Calliente Catering was attacked. That's a lot of coincidence. I don't believe in coincidence. Not in a murder investigation. And..." he hesitated as if for effect. "based on the fact that somebody turned that music off. Do you really think Pam Wickham turned the music off and then went to kill herself?"

Arno held Hal's stare for a long moment, making me think he was going to dig in his heels. But then he sighed. "You might be right. But my hands are tied on this. Sheriff Mulhern wants Wickham's death tied up in a tidy bow."

"What if you investigate it anyway?" I asked.

"To tell you the truth, I'm not sure. Mulhern's a walking temper tantrum lately."

"Worried about his friend?" Hal asked, a wry smile on his face.

Arno huffed out a laugh. "Among other things. He's

starting to look at running again. He doesn't want a lot of open cases staining his record."

"There *have* been a lot of murders in the area during his first term," I mumbled.

Arno leaned forward in his chair. "He's been threatening to cut all outside help in the office," he told Hal. "This is not the time to rock the boat."

Hal shook his head. "Do you want me to extricate myself from this?"

"That's not what I want at all. You have years more experience than the rest of my deputies. I count on your help for this type of thing. But I'm suggesting we might need to keep a lower profile."

He scanned me a hard look. "Maybe don't accost the mayor when he goes out for ice cream."

"Accost him?" I said, brows raised. "He was being very threatening to Karinne. I didn't want her to end up like the last woman who'd crossed him."

That woman had ended up dead. We hadn't been able to prove Robb was behind her death, but in my heart, I still believed he had something to do with it.

"Joey, that's just the kind of thing that will set Mulhern off. He doesn't need much of an excuse to cut Hal out of the work. You need to keep your nose out of this. You need to back off."

I glared at him, hating that he was right. "You want me to just look the other way if Robb's out of line?"

"Believe it or not, it's not your job to manage the mayor."

"Somebody has to do it!"

Arno growled in frustration. "Amity, you'd better get your girlfriend under control."

Unbelievably, Hal laughed. "You *have* met her, right?"

Arno shook his head.

"Look," Hal said. "I get that you're in a tough spot. But Joey's right. Robb was clearly threatening Karinne Magness. The woman was visibly shaken."

"Okay. Next time maybe call me? Or, if you don't have time to do that, at least use a little discretion. Maybe not unleash the five-foot-four-inch Kraken on him as your first salvo."

"Ha, ha," I mumbled.

Hal stood and offered Arno his hand. "I appreciate your support. I love helping out in Deer Hollow. But don't put your job on the line for me. If I'm cut loose, I can find my own work."

Arno stood and grabbed Hal's hand. "It's the principle of the thing. You've done quality work for me. I don't like that you're always the first to be blamed when something goes wrong."

Hal shrugged. "I'm an easy scapegoat. I have thick skin."

Arno nodded. "Thanks."

As we were leaving, Arno called out and Hal stopped, turning back.

"If worse comes to worst, I hear you have a booming career as a backup grill cook."

Hal gave him a long-suffering sigh, no doubt for Arno's entertainment. "I guess the gossip tree is in full bloom."

Arno finally smiled. "I know what you're doing even before you do it."

"I hope not," Hal said. "I'd hate to have to explain why we're going to have pie now, after eating ice cream earlier."

My pulse picked up with excitement. "Pie?" It was all I could do to keep from cackling with glee.

"Don't bother trying to explain. You're dating the carb queen. Just try to leave some pie for the rest of us."

That last part he'd directed at me. I winked, letting him

know there wasn't a chance I was leaving any pie for him. He was a turd. And if I had to buy five pies from Max, I'd make sure he'd have to go through me to get a slice.

If he thought Lis held a grudge, and she surely did, he was about to realize who the queen of grudges really was.

11

"**A**re you going to tell me why we're doing second dessert? I feel like a Hobbit." Hal threw me a disbelieving look. I hurried to clarify my point. "I'm not complaining, just curious."

"We've been told to lay low on this investigation."

"Yeah." I wasn't sure how me eating a big slice of banana cream pie had anything to do with laying low.

"We need to talk about the case, and if someone we needed to talk to anyway just happened to stop by the diner…"

It finally fell into place. "Ah. Stealth questioning?"

He shrugged. "You did it so well last night."

"Who are you hoping to see?"

"Karinne Magness knows more about all this than she's told us or the police."

I nodded. "Yes."

"Then there's this new donor Robb has been courting."

A single woman from Indianapolis? She'd probably eat late compared to our schedules. And there weren't that many restaurants in Deer Hollow. None that were open as late as Sonny's. I frowned. "But you're assuming she's still here. If she came for the party, she might be gone already."

"Except that Arno hasn't released any of the guests yet. She's supposed to stay in Deer Hollow until he tells her she can leave."

"But she's best buds with the mayor. If she wanted to leave, he'd surely step in on her behalf."

"It's possible."

I watched him closely, noting the relaxed and confident look on his handsome face. "But you don't think so. Why not?"

"Because I'm pretty sure she's staying at the Fawn Hotel." He parked at the curb in front of Sonny's Diner. A few cars away from his SUV was a smart little sports car that I didn't think belonged to anyone in Deer Hollow. I would have noticed that car. It probably cost as much as most Deer Hollowans made in a year.

I did remember seeing the car earlier, though. "I saw that car at the Fawn Hotel."

Coincidence? I didn't think so.

Hal climbed out and came around to help me down from the big car. He opened the door of the diner and I entered ahead of him. Mayor Robb's new donor was easy to spot. She sat in a booth in the back, her head down and her silky, white-blonde hair hiding her face. She was stunning. But her body language screamed that she wasn't looking for attention.

"Do you have a plan?" I asked Hal in a near-whisper.

He waved at Max, pointing to the booth next to our quarry's.

Max nodded. "I'll be there in five."

Placing a hand in the small of my back, Hal led me toward the booth. Fortunately for us, the diner was mostly empty. Besides the woman we were about to disturb and us, there was a guy who looked like he owned the big truck parked across the street and a couple of teens who appeared to be on a date. The teens had their heads together and wouldn't have noticed us if we'd set firecrackers off in our pants.

The truck driver was on his cell, probably checking in with the family he'd left behind when he hit the road.

Hal stopped next to the woman's table and she looked up, her clear blue gaze sliding over his tall form like an art connoisseur eyeing a newly discovered Picasso. She smiled, her hands fluttering over the tablet she'd been reading.

Hal gave her his one hundred twenty watt smile, and I'm pretty sure her ligaments all melted on the spot. "You were at Mayor Robb's party."

"I was." She nodded, her perfect skin pinkening as she finally spotted me. I read the extra color as embarrassment for having been caught ogling my boyfriend right in front of me.

I grinned. I couldn't blame a girl for looking. After all, the Greek deity was a sight to behold.

Hal offered her his hand. "I'm Hal Amity. This is Joey. Are you new to Deer Hollow?"

She shook her head, one slender hand sliding over the electronic device as if she were petting it. "I'm a friend of Martin Robb's." She held out a hand, fingers drooping as if she expected him to kiss the back of it. "Tiffany Brooks. It's a pleasure."

Hal took the offering, sandwiching it between both of his. "Tiffany. I'm sorry the party didn't turn out well. Did you know the victim?"

She closed her eyes and shook her head. "That poor man." The pretty blue eyes opened again, and she pointed to the other bench in her booth. "Why don't you sit with me."

"We don't want to interrupt," I said, motioning toward her tablet.

In response, she snapped the cover over it. "I hate to eat alone. This makes me feel less pathetic." Her laugh was light and genuine. "Please."

We slid into the booth. Tiffany pushed the tablet away as Max arrived with her dinner. It was a large salad with grilled chicken on top.

"What can I get you two?" Max asked.

"Pie?" we both said at once.

"Of course," she said, grinning.

"Is the pie good here?" Tiffany asked.

"Amazing," I told her. "It's well worth the calories."

Tiffany's eyes sparkled. "Good to know. I'll take a slice back to the hotel with me."

"I hope you found a nice place to stay," I nudged.

"It's gorgeous," she responded. "The view is stunning. I have a view of the river on two sides."

"You're on the South end then," Hal said, nodding. "It is stunning. Did you get the top floor?" He knew full well that Pam Wickham had the second-floor Vista room. But I assumed he was verifying Tiffany's location.

"First floor. Unfortunately, the top floor was already taken." She took a dainty bite of salad, chewing carefully before swallowing. "I hope you don't mind my eating. I'm starving."

"No, please," I gave her a grin. "We invaded your space."

"I'm glad you did. It's nice to have company."

"Have you known Martin long?" Hal asked.

Tiffany nodded, swallowing another bite. "Since college. We used to date." She laughed. "That was a long time ago."

"So, you're just friends now?" I asked.

She looked scandalized. "He's married."

"Yes, but..." I realized too late how cynical my next words were going to sound. "He and his wife aren't together anymore."

She frowned. "I heard what she did. It was all over the papers in Indy." Shaking her head, she tucked a strand of fine, straight hair behind a perfect ear. "To be honest, it was one of the reasons I decided to come down for the party. Poor Martin's been a mess about the whole thing." She dropped her fork into the bowl and made a face. "Unfortunately, I'm thinking he's in for it again."

"The body?" Hal nodded. "It's definitely not good that another body showed up in his home."

She leaned closer. "I saw you speaking to the Sheriff. Do you know who died?"

That was the moment I realized she'd wanted us to sit with her so she could pick Hal's brain about the murder. It made sense. There's a reason people gather around disasters. Human nature makes us naturally curious about that type of thing.

"His name was Jonathan Calliente. He owned the catering company."

Her eyes went wide. "I know Jonathan. Well..." she clarified. "I don't *know* know him. But we've met. Some of my friends use his catering services in Indianapolis." She nibbled some lettuce, her pretty face creasing into a frown.

Max placed pie in front of Hal and me. "Enjoy."

"What's wrong?" Hal asked Tiffany after Max had left.

"What? Oh. I was just remembering that Mr. Calliente wasn't very popular with some of his clients. He tended to bill more than he said his services would cost. Maybe that's why he was working out here in the..." She stopped, her face flushing again. "Sorry. I'm a died-in-the-wool city girl."

I laughed. "No worries. Bumpkinville isn't for everybody."

She gave a less than ladylike snort at that. "Bumpkinville. That's wonderful." She cocked her head. "Do you like it here?"

"I'd never live anywhere else. It's an entirely different lifestyle. One that suits me."

She chewed thoughtfully. "I can see the charm. But I'd miss the shopping and the shows."

I fake-frowned. "Clearly, you haven't experienced Junior's Market. Once you've been in there, you'll never want to shop again."

She threw back her head and laughed. "I like you, Joey."

I liked her too. "Ditto."

"Tell me about yourself."

Twenty minutes later, she was wiping tears from her eyes and declaring she needed a pig, a dog, and a cat.

"There's never a dull moment," I agreed.

Tiffany glanced at her diamond-studded gold watch. "It's late. I should be going." She turned to flag Max down and ordered a piece of pie to go. "I can't wait to try it," she said with a wide smile.

Hal leaned forward. "Before you go, I wonder if you could answer a couple more questions for me?"

"Sure."

"Did you by any chance meet the woman in the room above yours?"

"No. Should I have?"

"Not necessarily. But you might have recognized her if you had. Her name was Pam Wickham. She was Jonathan Calliente's fiancé."

Understanding slowly lit Tiffany's eyes. "She worked in the business too."

"Yes. They were partners."

"Ah. Poor woman. No, I never met her. But I'll stop up and give her my regrets in the morning."

"She's no longer there," Hal said.

"Oh?"

"I wonder, did you happen to notice anybody visiting her earlier today? Or hear any noises coming from above?"

Tiffany thought about it. "There was some thumping around lunchtime. I thought I might have heard a short scream, but Martin told me it was probably just the television." Her expression tightened with concern. "Did something happen to her?"

"I'm afraid so."

She frowned. "Somebody was playing music above me. It was loud. I complained once, and it went quiet a little after that." She placed a hand over her mouth. "Was she killed?"

"Around noon."

Tiffany made a small sound of horror, and tears filled her eyes. "I heard her. I might have saved her."

"You couldn't have known," I said, reaching across the table to clasp her hand.

"I'm surprised you didn't hear the sirens and see all the police cars," Hal told her.

"When were they there?"

"We found the body around six o'clock. The police arrived twenty minutes later."

She stared at Hal. "I was running along the river about that time. The water is rushing and it's pretty loud. There *was* one police car still parked in the lot when I got back, but

I just assumed it was somebody who was staying at the hotel."

"How far did you run?" I asked, curious.

"Three miles, give or take. But I stopped and sat by the water for about an hour, just thinking. I find the sheer power of the water fascinating."

I laughed. "I'm impressed. I'd drop dead if I ran more than a mile."

She gave me a sad smile, shaking her head. "Running makes my world seem less crazy. It calms me."

"How long was the mayor at the hotel with you?" Hal's tone was soft, his manner non-confrontational, but I saw Tiffany stiffen just the same.

"You think we're having an affair." It wasn't a question, and the guilty way her gaze kept sliding away told me there might be some truth in it.

She shook her head as if she'd read my mind. "We're not." She frowned. "Martin would like it to be something, but I really can't let that happen."

"Why not?" I asked.

She appeared surprised by my question. "He's a married man."

I nodded, understanding why that would be a problem for her. It would be for me. Even if his wife was in prison. But I had to wonder if that was the only reason.

Tiffany's shoulders loosened when she realized we weren't going to press her on the situation. She sighed. "I know how it looks. And, if I'm being honest, I was tempted. Martin and I had a good thing in college. But he's different now. And I've pretty much stayed the same."

I nodded toward the diamond band on her left hand. "You got married too."

To my surprise, she barked out an almost angry laugh.

"Divorced. The marriage barely outlasted the wedding." She ran a finger over the sparkling stones on her ring. "I wear this just so men will leave me alone. I'm not interested in anything but friendship right now."

"What time did Mayor Robb leave the hotel?" Hal asked.

She blinked, clearly surprised. "You don't think he killed that woman?"

"I haven't formed an opinion on anything yet," Hal told her with a smile that was meant to soothe. "I'm simply getting as many facts as I can."

She nodded. "He left a little while after the music stopped upstairs. Maybe twelve-thirty? It wasn't much after that, anyway."

Hal handed her a card. "If you think of anything else. Anything at all, will you call me?"

"Of course."

We climbed to our feet and watched Tiffany walk out of the diner. She seemed genuinely upset. Given the fact that she'd been in the vicinity of back-to-back murders, it made perfect sense. "She'll probably get in her car and start driving back to Indy tonight. I wouldn't blame her."

Hal nodded. "I wouldn't blame her either. But I hope she doesn't."

I glanced at him and was surprised to see speculation painting his expression. "What is it?"

"I'm not sure," he responded. "But what are the chances that Tiffany Brooks would be within spitting distance of two murders and not be somehow connected?"

That thought made me frown. "Not good?"

He wrapped an arm around me and tugged me close.

"Not good at all."

12

_____

We had a surprise waiting for us when we walked out of Sonny's. A big man, exuding strength and power despite being in his mid-fifties, leaned against a cream-colored SUV with the sheriff's logo on the side. It was parked next to Hal's Escalade.

His muscular arms crossed over his chest, Sheriff Mulhern straightened and shoved his hands in the pockets of his jeans, his dark brown gaze tracking us as we approached.

Mulhern extended his hand to Hal, giving us a wide smile that showed a lot of very white teeth. "Amity." He looked my way and doffed his cowboy hat in an old-fashioned move that I was sure was meant to be charming. I was a little charmed. But I knew too much about the sheriff to be totally taken in by the act. "Miss Joey Fulle. It's a pleasure to run into you. How's your mom doing?"

I gave him back a smile I hoped looked more genuine than it felt on my face. "She and Garland are in Paris. Last I heard, they were having the time of their lives."

His smile dimmed. If I hadn't been watching for it, I

would probably have missed it. Message sent and received. He needed to be reminded that, although he had some powerful friends, so did I.

"If you want food, you'd better hurry," Hal said amiably. "Max will be closing down the grill soon."

Mulhern's grin turned a little mean around the edges. "Spoken like a man who's worked the grill."

Hal laughed. "I have, and I'll admit it was eye-opening. People who work in a restaurant deserve a lot of credit. Their jobs are hard, and they put up with a lot of guff they don't deserve."

I patted him on the back. "That guy was a jerk," I told him. "And I totally disagree. You do know how to burn a perfectly good burger."

Mulhern laughed. "I'll remember your words of wisdom the next time I'm at a restaurant."

Hal inclined his head. "What can I help you with tonight, Sheriff?"

The cop leaned back against his car again, crossing his legs at the ankles as he appeared to be considering what he wanted to say. Finally, he scrubbed a big hand over his face. When he looked up again, his expression was classic regret. Mulhern was quite the thespian. "I don't want you to think this is personal." He skimmed his faux despair in my direction. I held his gaze, giving nothing away. "I just can't have you going around harassing the people of Deer Hollow. I have residents callin' me to complain that people without a badge are grillin' them about stuff."

"Really?" Hal wore a slight smile. "That surprises me. I don't think I've annoyed anybody recently."

Arms crossed over my chest, I avoided the sheriff's gaze as my blood began to boil. I knew what he was building up to, and it was beyond unfair. I kept my gaze on his chest, focused on a black spot on the collar of his uniform shirt near the pocket. It looked like he'd jammed an open sharpie into his pocket.

Mulhern ignored Hal's remark. "Then there's the budget concerns. I can't continue to justify payin' an outsider to do the work my deputies should do."

Hal nodded, hands on hips. "I'm glad to hear you're going to hire some more deputies. I'm sure your people will be relieved. Their workload is exhausting."

Mulhern's fake smile slid completely away. His jaw tightened. "You're not tellin' me how to run my office, are you, Amity?"

"Somebody needs to," I said before I could stop myself. "Hal's got the background and skill to really do you some good. I have to wonder why you wouldn't want to accept help from him."

"Joey," Hal warned softly.

I placed a hand on his arm. "I'll shut up now. But that needed to be said." I turned and walked away, climbing into Hal's car and slamming the door before my big mouth got Hal in trouble. I watched the two men for another minute, seething, and then glared at Mulhern through the window as Hal headed around the car.

When he slipped behind the wheel, I turned to him, arching a brow in question.

"I wonder what's put the bee in his britches about our investigation," Hal murmured.

"A massive brain malfunction?"

Hal laughed. To my surprise, he didn't seem all that upset about being fired. When I said as much to him, he shrugged. "It's been coming for a while. At least the separation should take Arno out of the line of fire."

"What now?" I asked.

"Now, we keep moving forward. I'm a PI. I don't need the sheriff's permission to do my job."

I grinned. "I'm sensing another dollar bill in your immediate future."

He backed out of the spot and headed toward home. "Just a dollar? I'm pretty sure I'm worth at least five."

"Oh," I said with feeling, "You're worth at least six or seven."

His laughter took some of the tightness from my shoulders, but that still left me with an ache in my heart for what Mulhern's tricks might do to my PI and me on a personal level. Hal couldn't survive very long if I was the only one paying him. And his pride wouldn't let that happen anyway.

But if the sheriff kept him from getting jobs in the area, Hal would have to return to Indianapolis full time. And that thought made my heart hurt.

HAL WALKED me to my front door and gave me a kiss that made my knees melt. As he broke the kiss, I sighed. "No wonder I keep hiring you as my PI. You have mad skills."

Tugging a strand of my hair, he laughed. "I'm going to assume you mean my dogged persistence and ability to ferret out even the smallest detail of a tough case."

I let my lips curl into a slow smile. "You can go ahead and assume. But you know what they say about that."

He gave me a quick kiss and turned toward the steps. "I'll be over in the morning to cook you breakfast."

My smile widened. "Now you're talking my language. Give little Miss Piggy a kiss for me."

"I will. Tell the Beauty I've got a tennis ball with her

name on it for tomorrow." He opened the car door and grinned at me. "I found some hot pink ones."

"She'll love it." The pibl didn't really care what color the balls were. She only cared that her second favorite person in all the world was throwing them for her.

I waited until Hal's car left the drive before opening the front door. Caphy didn't make a habit of chasing cars into the road, but if she knew Hal was in the car, she might do the unthinkable. Still, as I turned the key in the lock, I thought she might peel a few inches of wood off the inside before I got it open.

I stepped aside as I pushed it open and she shot past me, spun on her heels at the stairs, and came thundering back to swipe a wet kiss over my ankle before tearing off into the yard to do her business.

"Meow!"

A soft warmth pressed against my calves. I looked down to find LaLee twining around my legs. "Hey, Diva." I bent to scratch under her chin.

She thanked me by putting her teeth on my hand and then stalking back into the house, her long tail beating a rat, tat, tat against the air.

"Fickle feline," I mumbled.

My cell rang, and I dug it out of my pocket. I didn't recognize the number and almost didn't answer it. But I was a glutton for punishment, so I did. "Hello?"

"Is this Joey Fulle?"

I frowned. "Who's calling?" I made it a practice not to give out information unless I knew who I was giving it to. Not even my name.

"Mayor Robb has bad things in his past and dangerous friends. Watch your step."

The call disconnected and I stared at it, shocked and

chilled by the urgently whispered message. "What just happened?" I mumbled to myself.

Suddenly chilled, I called Caphy and went into the house, locking the door after the pitty joined me. I briefly considered calling Hal and telling him about the call, but it was late, and the caller really hadn't told me anything I didn't already know.

Except for the part about Robb having dangerous friends. What had the caller meant by that?

When the phone rang again, I jumped, my heart pounding against my ribs. But a quick glance at the screen told me I had nothing to fear. I hit the answer button. "Hey, Lis. What are you doing up so late?"

Since retiring from the modeling world, my bestie had become an early-to-rise, early-to-bed type of gal. It was rare for her to call me after nine pm.

"Hey, girlfriend. I'm sorry to call so late."

"It's okay. I just got home. What's up?"

"It's maybe nothing, but I was showing a house across the street from the diner tonight, and I saw you and Hal go inside."

"You should have come over and had pie with us."

"I couldn't. This couple I'm working with is going to be the death of me. They're first-time buyers who don't want to spend a lot of money, but they want everything. Granite countertops, massive rooms, a swimming pool, blah, blah, blah."

I laughed. I'd seen enough of those home-buying shows to know exactly the type she meant.

"To make things worse, the husband wants a traditional style, and the wife wants contemporary. And they both work until seven-thirty, so all of our appointments are late."

She sighed. "I'm exhausted."

"Poor baby. I feel your pain. It sounds like you need a girl's weekend in Indianapolis. I'm sure Felly would love to join us."

Felicity Chance was my cousin. Felly lived about an hour away in Indianapolis. The three of us had fun together no matter what we did, even if we just stayed inside, watched Rom Coms together, and ate too much.

"That sounds perfect! But it'll have to wait until next weekend, I'm afraid. I'm booked solid through this weekend and all next week."

"It's a date."

"Anyway, I got distracted. The reason I called was..." She hesitated. "I'm probably being stupid, but..."

"Lis, spit it out. I'm growing roots here."

"I'm pretty sure you were being followed tonight."

Any inclination to tease her died on my lips. "Followed? What do you mean?"

"When you guys parked and went into the diner, a car pulled up across the street and sat there. The guy inside didn't leave the car. And he was staring at the diner for a long time."

I tried to remember if there'd been a car across the street when we came out of Sonny's. I didn't remember any, but I'd been focused on Sheriff Mulhern. "Was it still there when we left?"

"No, that's the thing. When the sheriff pulled into a spot next to yours, the guy left so fast I'm surprised he didn't leave skid marks on the road."

Ice crawled through my chest. "Maybe he was there for someone else."

"It's possible, I guess. But he arrived when you did." I could picture her shrugging, her tone filled with doubt. "It might be nothing, but I just wanted to tell you to be careful."

Given that she was the second person in moments to warn me, I was starting to think it was a good idea.

"What did the car look like?"

"Small, white. Kind of a clunker. I didn't recognize it."

The ice in my chest thickened, making it hard to breathe. "Was there a sticker on the back bumper? It would have been half torn off, but there was a silver swirl and the word *Success* still visible?"

"I couldn't read the sticker, but I noticed it as headlights from the passing cars flashed over it. The silver glowed in the light. I know that sticker. I remember it from when Mayor Robb was campaigning. If I remember right, the slogan was, Safety, Security..."

"Success," I finished for her. Of course! The swirl I'd envisioned wasn't a swirl at all. It was kind of an artsy-fartsy representation of a mystical Deer Hollow that existed only in the new mayor's strange mind. When I'd first seen that logo, I'd thought it looked more like Indi-anapolis than Deer Hollow. Hal and I had speculated that Robb hadn't bothered to invest in a new emblem but had just used the logo he'd created when he ran for Indy city council.

I dropped my face into my hands. "I'm being stalked by one of Mayor Robb's fanboys?"

Lis laughed at my characterization. "Not necessarily." The smile in her voice slid away. "The thing is, I think I've seen the driver before."

"Where?"

"Do you remember when you got that phantom call from the guy who took Hal's phone in the Bend Over and Coffee?"

The Bend Over and Coffee was a new shop in town, owned by the wife of a proctologist. The place was wildly popular because of its funny name, great coffee, and excellent pastries.

I thought about that guy. Arno had described him as around thirty, five eleven-ish, kind of wiry with wavy, reddish-brown hair. "Coffee house guy," I said, frowning. "But you never saw him, did you?"

"I didn't." There was a long silence. "But the description stuck with me because it was as if he was describing somebody I'd known all my life."

"Who?" I was getting excited. Maybe we knew the killer. Maybe we could put a pin in the investigation, and Hal could prove once again how valuable an asset he was to the sheriff's department.

"Joey, I can't believe you haven't put the pieces together. It was someone you've known all your life too."

I was tired and just wanted to go to bed. But Lis's information was important. Still, I wasn't in the mood to be scolded. I might have been a little curt in my response to my bestie. "How would I recognize a description of some random dude I've never met?"

"Because it describes your father perfectly," she said in a soft, achingly kind voice. "And the guy I saw in that car looked enough like your dad to be related."

I was suddenly cold, as if the temperature in the room had plummeted. My knees gave out and dropped me to the steps leading to the second floor. In that moment, I wasn't sure I'd even have the strength to make it upstairs. "It was my dad?"

"No, Joey. I'm sorry. I don't want to give you false hope. This guy was much too young to be your dad. But, Joe, he could easily be your brother."

"I have a brother?" My voice was small, pathetic. "That's not possible. My mother would have told me."

"Maybe he's a cousin or something. Maybe he's your dad's younger doppelganger. I..." She sighed. "I hope I didn't just make a terrible mistake. But I thought you should know."

"No, you were right to tell me. I'm sure he's not related. But it sounds like he's involved in this case somehow."

"Okay." She sounded relieved. "I'll let you get to bed. Talk soon?"

"Of course." I hung up and sat there, staring toward the front door with my thoughts simmering. A brother? I rolled the idea over in my mind for a few minutes and realized I wouldn't mind it at all. Not one little bit.

When I realized I was smiling, I shook it off. "I don't have a brother," I scolded myself. But I might have a suspect. Heading up the stairs to my room, I thought again about calling Hal. Again, I decided against it. He was coming to breakfast. I'd tell him then.

And with that happy thought, I quickly got ready for bed and slipped beneath the cool, smooth sheets. Caphy jumped up and sprawled across her usual spot at the bottom of the bed. LaLee was already asleep on my extra pillow, belly up and long legs sticking into the air.

I grinned at her, gave her irresistible tummy a scratch, and then took a deep breath, settling down to sleep.

13

"Thanks for breakfast," I told my PI.

He grinned. "It was my pleasure. I'm sorry you didn't get more of it."

I snorted out a laugh. "Why don't any of the little rats beg food from you?"

Caphy shifted on the back seat of the car and grinned at me, tongue lolling. Her muscular tail beat an excited rhythm against the back of the seat.

Hal glanced at her sweet face in the rearview mirror, his lips twitching. "They know I won't give it to them." He said it smugly, punctuating it with a slight tilt upward of his strong chin. I fought a grin, not wanting to burst his smug bubble. Hal liked to think of himself as the disciplinarian of the two of us. But he was just a big softie at heart.

I'd seen him sneaking bites of egg to Ethel and Caphy before breakfast. And LaLee had been suspiciously friendly to him when he was putting things away in the fridge.

Friendly, like she thought he was going to feed her. Or already had. The diva was never friendly to Hal unless she thought it would buy her something.

"How are we going to know which maid to talk to?" I asked Hal as we neared the Fawn Hotel.

"Work schedules," he said. "There can't be more than two or three maids working at a time in a place this size. One of them has to be our maid."

That made sense. We'd discussed it over breakfast, deciding that since both the sheriff and Tiffany had mentioned a maid around the time Pam Wickham was killed, it was an open switch we needed to close.

"What do you think about the guy who might have been following us last night?" I asked the Greek deity.

Hal frowned. "It's an interesting development. Especially the car aspect. Whoever this guy is, he was at the scene of Prince's attack too. That's too much coincidence for me."

"Yeah, me too. He's part of this mess. Somehow." I thought about it. "Do you remember a server at Robb's party that fits the description?"

"Not really." He thought about it for a beat and then selected Arno's cell number from his recent call list. The cop answered after two rings. He sounded wary. "Amity."

"Hey," Hal responded, his tone light.

Caphy barked at the sound of Arno's voice. She shoved her squishy head over the back of my seat and rested it on my shoulder.

"Hi, Caphy. Joey." Arno said, a smile in his voice.

I frowned at the screen and said nothing. I was still peeved about Hal's ouster.

"I was wondering if you could get me a list and stats for the catering company's servers at the party?" Hal said. "Photos would be good too."

There was a beat of silence before Arno cleared his throat. "I thought the sheriff spoke to you."

"He did."

Another pulse of silence. "Okay. I'll forward those files to you."

"Great," Hal said.

"No problem. But, listen, Hal, I'm sure I don't have to tell you…"

"What files?" Hal said.

"Right," Arno sounded relieved. "Look, I'm sorry about…" he seemed to be struggling with the words. "I should have warned you."

"Mulhern told you to keep quiet and stay away from me, didn't he?"

"Well, yeah, but…"

"Then it's best if he *knows* you're staying away from me. Except on a personal level. Right?"

Arno expelled a relieved breath. "Thanks for understanding."

"Don't think anything of it," Hal said, a wicked grin on his face. "Just make sure you're deaf, dumb, and blind when I continue to work this case."

Laughing, Arno said, "Are you on a cell phone? You're breaking up. I can't hear you. Gotta go."

Hal disconnected, and we sat in silence for a moment. Despite Hal's easy acceptance of what had to feel a little like Arno's betrayal, I was more than a little annoyed with my friend, the cop. Despite what Mulhern told Arno, he should have warned Hal what was coming.

Hal reached over and squeezed my hand, his grip warm and comforting. "He had to do what he was told, honey."

I blew air through my lips, frowning.

"It won't help me if he gets fired."

"Mulhern wouldn't fire Arno. If he did, he might have to do some actual work himself. That'll never happen."

"He could always promote one of the other deputies."

"If he did, his solved case percentage would plummet, and he knows it. As annoying as he is, Arno's a good cop. And he makes people feel safe. The others are either too new or don't have the leadership experience."

"Schmidt could do it," Hal said.

I nodded. Deputy Kim Schmidt had only been at the sheriff's office for a few months, but I was pretty sure she'd been a cop for several years. "Mulhern would never promote Schmidt." It was sad but true. Mulhern didn't respect women enough to give Schmidt that kind of power. "Besides, Sheppard's been there longer than Schmidt."

Hal pulled into the parking lot of the Fawn Hotel and shot me a grin. I burst into laughter with him. Deputy Mark Sheppard was a micro-cop with a larger-than-life persona. Whoever coined the term, short man syndrome must have known Sheppard. At five feet four, I stood head to head with the man, and I was pretty sure my arms were bigger around than his legs. He was a decent cop, tenacious as all get-out, but he had enough weirdness in his personality to sink a small battleship. Or a small sheriff's office.

"Arno's safe for now," I told Hal. "Unless Mulhern brings in someone with rank from Indianapolis."

"Yeah, that's always a possibility."

Hal parked near the office and we climbed out. I stretched the stiffness out of my body and closed my eyes, enjoying the feel of the morning sun on my face and shoulders. The constant rush of the Fawn River was a familiar sound that would quickly become white noise if we stood outside for long.

The hotel consisted of two levels, all exterior doors, with about twenty rooms on each level. Though it was early summer, none of the guesthouses in town were full. That would happen in a couple of months when the weather was hot, and Deer Hollow and the surrounding towns all had their festivals.

A door opened on the second floor and a woman came out, her white cotton uniform immediately identifying her as one of our targets.

Hal put his hand in the small of my back, and we headed for the nearby stairs. By the time we'd reached the top floor, the woman had gone back inside the room. The sound of vacuuming filled the air. A cart filled with clean towels, linens, and extra supplies waited near the wall to one side of the open door.

Hal knocked on the door frame and stuck his head inside. "Hello?"

The maid came out of the bathroom, holding a bundle of towels. "Sí?"

I stepped through the door. "Hello. How are you?"

The woman's round face creased with worry.

Hal held his credentials up so she could see them. "We're investigating the death next door. We were wondering if we could ask you a few questions?"

The maid looked from Hal to me, her brown eyes going wide as she took in his PI credentials. That tag above her left breast said her name was Alda Rodriquez. Her warm brown skin paled, and she shook her head. "I not know."

At first, I thought she was proclaiming that she wasn't sure she wanted to answer questions. But, as she backed away, her pretty brown eyes wide with terror, I realized the problem ran deeper than that.

"Alda, my name is Joey. I promise we only want to know what you saw yesterday. Can you help us? A woman died, and we're trying to find out why and who did it?"

Alda stopped backtracking, but she still clutched the

mound of towels against her belly like a shield. After another moment of indecision, she nodded. "Sí."

Hal smiled. "Thank you. Can you tell us who was in the room next door around noon yesterday?"

Alda frowned again. I was starting to suspect we might have a language barrier.

"She can't tell you anything," a cool female voice said from behind us. Hal and I turned around to find a woman striding toward us from the other end of the building. She wore her straight brown hair in a sharp, chin-length bob that wasn't very flattering on her narrow face. Her chin was long and slightly pointed, her mouth a thin slash across the bottom of her face. She had a wide nose, which turned up slightly at the end.

The most attractive thing about her were her eyes. They were golden brown, and the lashes surrounding them were thick and long.

She offered Hal her hand as she reached us, her unsmiling countenance swinging from him to me. "I'm Victoria Lass, the manager of this hotel."

We introduced ourselves again, and Hal showed her his credentials.

After examining the laminated badge, Ms. Lass turned to the maid. "Estas personas son amigas, Alda. Por favor, responda a sus preguntas."

The young maid blinked rapidly and then nodded, chewing her bottom lip.

"What did you tell her?" I asked.

"That you are friends, and she should answer your questions." Her narrow lips curved in a self-deprecating smile. "My Spanish is only barely passable. But I can usually get the message across."

I found the "friends" comment odd. "Thank you."

Lass inclined her head. "When I told him about the murder, Garland told me you'd probably stop by."

Ahh. That explained it.

Hal turned to the young maid again. "Can you tell us who was in the room yesterday around lunchtime?"

Lass turned to Alda. "¿Quién estaba en la habitación cuando murió la mujer?"

The girl shook her head. "No vi."

"She didn't see anybody," Victoria Lass translated.

"Did she hear anything?" Hal asked.

Victoria pointed to her ear. "¿Escuchaste algo?"

"¡Sí!" Alda nodded vigorously. "Música."

"Did you see anyone leave the room after the music was turned off?" Hal asked the maid.

We waited as Victoria translated the question and watched the girl frown, then give us a firm shake of the head.

"You didn't see the woman who was staying there leave?" I asked.

After the translation of my question, Aldo shook her head again. Her gaze wouldn't meet mine or Hal's, and her posture was about as closed up as it could get.

Victoria Lass sighed. "She's afraid of something. But she says she didn't see anybody leave."

"Is it possible the killer threatened her?" I asked.

Victoria shrugged her bony shoulders. "It's possible. Alda's here on a work visa, but she lives in fear she'll lose it. She doesn't trust authority figures."

"Sheriff Mulhern was apparently here to check on the noise complaint.," Hal said. "He spoke to a maid. Was there anybody else working yesterday who might have talked to him?"

"I'm afraid not, Mr. Amity. Only a dozen of the rooms are

currently in use. I don't need more than one maid right now. Alda is on the schedule for all of this week."

"Is it possible she spoke to him and doesn't want to tell us?"

"Anything's possible. She's a sweet girl, but she is very timid. I'm sorry we couldn't be of more help."

"I'd like to see the feeds from your security cameras, please."

"Of course. Just stop by the office before you leave. What else can I help with?"

"Can you let us into the victim's room?"

Without hesitation, Victoria pulled a coil of plastic off her slim wrist and handed it to him. The coil contained several access cards. "The silver one is a master. I'll be in the office when you're ready to view the security footage."

"Thanks," I said.

"My pleasure. I love my job here, Ms. Fulle. Mr. Medford is a wonderful boss. And your mother is full of surprises." She said that last with a fondness that told me the surprises were a good thing.

I grinned. "Thank you. She's definitely that."

As Victoria Lass headed back to her office, Hal and I went to the last room on the upper floor. A wide X of yellow crime scene tape still decorated the freshly painted navy blue door.

Hal used the key to open the door and then motioned for me to stay back while he cleared the room. He slipped between the sections of tape, leaving them intact, and disappeared into the room, gun drawn. The care with which he'd preserved the barrier reminded me that we were supposed to be off the case.

I stared at the boiling waters of the Fawn while I waited. The river cut a winding path through a towering cliff of rock on the far side and a verdant and well-maintained acre of grass, trees, and flowers on the hotel side. Garland had done a lot of landscaping work since the last time I'd been there.

Well, the second to the last time. The last time had been less than twenty-four hours earlier. When we found a corpse hanging from the balcony.

I was pretty sure that hadn't been part of Garland's planned improvements.

With the river roaring past, I barely heard the shout from inside the room. Responding a beat too late, I spun and stepped toward the door.

A figure burst from the room, smashing right through the tape, and jerked with surprise when he encountered me.

I jolted to a stop, my eyes going wide.

He did a graceful sidestep, hesitating only a millisecond as his gaze met mine. The gray-blue eyes, so familiar, widened slightly. Time seemed to stand still, stretching the impossibly short moment into something long enough to twist my stomach and steal the breath from my lungs.

It was long enough to know that Lis had been right.

"Who...?"

I never got to finish that question. In the blink of an eye, he was over the railing and gone. I heard a grunt and a thump and then footsteps pounding over the boardwalk that ran along the building on the lower level.

Gun drawn, Hal burst from the room and fixed me with a slightly wild gaze. "Where'd he go?"

I just stared at my PI, too flummoxed to answer.

"Joey?" He lowered the gun and approached, one hand finding my arm and giving it a squeeze. "Honey, what's wrong?"

I shook my head. My eyes felt as if they were the size of golf balls.

Hal's handsome face tightened with worry. "Joey, honey, you're scaring me. Are you hurt?"

I shook my head, finally sliding my gaze to his. "I…"

His hands cupped my face. He lowered his head to look me in the eyes. "Talk to me. What is it?"

A single tear slipped down my cheek. "I…" Swallowing the lump forming in my throat, I fixed him with a disbelieving look. "I think I just saw my brother."

14

As promised, Victoria Lass was waiting for us in the hotel's common area. Her plain face held an expression of concern, and her footfalls sounded almost angry as she strode toward us.

I glanced around with appreciative surprise. As with everything he'd accomplished in the refurbished hotel, Garland had done an excellent job with the hotel's lobby area.

The ceiling was higher than I'd expected, making the not-oversized space feel much larger than it was. A loft ran the length of the riverside wall. It held several seating areas of comfortable chairs that were facing a large TV nestled in the middle of several shelves of books.

The floors were light wood, either ash or maple, I wasn't sure which, and scattered with brightly-colored rugs sporting Native American prints. The long, outside wall was comprised of sliding doors and windows, with an inviting patio beyond the glass and a view of the river beyond that. Decorative lanterns strung around the patio made it a welcoming spot for pleasant evenings imbibing drinks from the coffee and cocktail bar tucked under the loft.

The seating in front of the windows was similar to that in the loft, overstuffed and covered in what looked like a soft tweed fabric.

Hal inclined his chin. "Ms. Lass. Did you get a chance to set up a viewing of the security tapes?"

She motioned toward the counter that ran along one side of the surprisingly bright space. "I've set it up in my office. It's just through here."

A young girl stood behind the counter, her eyes wide as we filed past her and through a door, entering an office that was furnished much like the main space. "Tanya, you're in charge for the next few minutes."

The young girl watched us like a hawk as we entered her boss's office, speculation clear in her deep-set eyes.

Victoria Lass went around behind her desk and turned her all-in-one computer around so we could see the monitor. "Since you think Ms. Wickham was killed around midday, I queued up the footage from eleven AM until one PM. I've sped it up considerably. Let me know if you want me to slow anything down."

We watched several cars come in and out of the lot. Most of them parked in front of the building, the drivers going directly to their rooms. As expected, Sheriff Mulhern drove in a little after eleven-thirty to answer the loud music charge and headed up the stairs. Unfortunately, the lot cameras didn't catch the upper floor of the lodgings.

The sheriff left around eleven fifty-five, which would have given him enough time to knock on the door several times and then speak briefly with the maid.

When we reached the one o'clock mark, Hal looked at Victoria. "I think we're done with the lot footage."

But I saw a flash of something just on the outside edge of the footage. "Wait," I placed a hand on Hal's arm. "Can you slow that to normal and replay the last minute?"

Victoria nodded and complied.

I watched a silver sedan drive into the lot and move toward the middle of the lodgings. The car drove slowly past a large willow tree on the edge of the lot, and I saw what I'd thought I'd seen behind it. "There!" I pointed toward the front end of a small car.

"Stop it there, please?" Hal requested.

"We moved closer and peered at the image. It could be the car I saw when we found Prince."

Hal glanced at the manager. "Can you enlarge this at all?"

"Not much. It will get too pixelated." She tapped her keyboard, and the feed scrolled rapidly backward, the clock in the upper corner flashing numbers at a speed that was almost too fast to follow.

Two hours passed, and she stopped it as the little white car I remembered drove into the lot and backed beneath the drooping branches of the willow.

We scrolled through it several times but couldn't see the driver in any of the pictures.

Hal looked at me. "Is that the car?"

"Yes."

Hal nodded. "Can we get a few pictures of this car? And then I'd like to see the upper floor."

Her expression tightened, and her mouth thinned. "I'm afraid there's a problem with that."

She changed perspective, and the screen went black.

We didn't react. I was thinking the software was in flux and would settle onto the correct perspective any second. But it remained black.

Hal and I swung our gazes to Victoria at the same time. Her eyes as hard as pebbles, she held out a cell phone. "This is what those cameras look like."

I stared with horror at a monitoring device whose lens was coated in a glossy black substance. The paint coated its face and dripped down its sides.

"What about the footage directly before this?"

Victoria scanned it back several moments. The camera was working, the picture clear and sharp. And then a black splatter blocked out part of the image. Followed by a heavier wash of obscuring paint. And the image was gone.

"There's no footage of anyone walking up to it?"

Victoria shook her head. "Not a soul."

"How did someone paint this without being seen?" I asked.

Victoria nodded at my question. "I've been thinking about that. The way the railings are on the ends of the decking, someone who was agile could have climbed up behind the camera and painted it without being seen."

"How about from the camera on the other end?"

"It's clear. It captured everything up to a little over halfway down the decking. But it didn't catch any activity beyond that."

I frowned, thinking about someone painting over a camera in broad daylight. "Can you go back to the parking lot footage and pan it forward to within an hour of the sheriff's arrival?"

She did as I requested, and we watched Martin Robb drive into the lot and park in front of Tiffany Brooks' room. Before disappearing beneath the upper balcony, he glanced up at the room above Tiffany's. Did he know who was in that room? Or, had he been looking at the camera that hung from the corner of the roof? The one that ended up covered in black paint?

Hal and I shared a look. "Why would he be so interested in the camera on the top floor?" I asked.

"That's an excellent question," Hal said. "The answer requires another conversation with Mayor Robb."

"Could you tell if anything was disturbed?" Arno asked, his body language as taut as I'd ever seen it. If I had to guess, I'd say Sheriff Mulhern was putting a lot of pressure on him to close the Calliente investigation.

"The scene looked the same as I remembered it," Hal told him. "Did your people get any new fingerprints?"

Arno ran a hand through his blond hair, leaving it standing up on end at the top. "They're working on it now." He fixed me with a look, his brown eyes trying to drill into my head and find the answers he hadn't been able to wring from me. "Joey, this is bad. If this guy is really related to you, Mulhern's going to do more than ask you to leave the case. He'll arrest you for tampering with evidence."

I just shook my head, too dazed and confused to respond.

Out of the corner of my eye, I saw Arno glance at Hal for help.

My PI shook his head. "Give her a break, Arno. We don't even know who this guy is yet. If we could get fingerprints that may actually be a good thing. If his prints are on file and we discover he's a known entity, that might help us find him and clear all of this up."

"And if they're not?" I asked, surprised at the sound of my own voice. I hadn't intended to speak until I had a chance to talk to my mom. I wanted to know if it was possible I had a brother.

Hal squeezed my shoulder. "Then he hasn't been in trouble before, and that will work in our favor." He crouched down in front of me, clasping my icy hands in his. "Either way, we'll get to the bottom of this, honey."

I believed him. He was a man who pursued knowledge with dogged persistence, never giving up until he found his answers. But, I was caught in a weird limbo between joy at the idea of having a brother and fear that he was apparently mixed up in a murder.

I nodded mutely. "I need to try to reach Joline," I told him.

Hal stood and pulled me gently to my feet. Glancing at Arno, he said, "Let me know if you learn anything about the guy?"

Arno nodded.

We headed for the door.

Arno's voice stopped us as I was stepping into the hall-way. "You said this guy drove the white car you saw leaving the scene of Mr. Prince's attack?"

I nodded. "He was driving it last night too. Apparently, he was following us."

Arno's gaze tightened, narrowed. "And you know this how?"

I briefly debated not telling him but figured he'd have to handle his own problems with Lis. I had enough problems of my own. "Lis was showing a house across the street from Sonny's. She saw him watching us."

Arno's gaze swung away, and he nodded. "Okay. Thanks."

I glanced at Hal. That had been way too easy. "Tell her I'll call later," I told Arno.

He didn't glance up. He just shook his head.

"Let's head home," Hal said as we exited the building. "You can make your call, and I'll fix us something to eat."

That was a deal I couldn't refuse.

The silence between us was uncomfortable as we drove home. Hal glanced at me a few times. I knew he was worried, but I needed time to process what I'd seen, and I couldn't reassure him until I had.

He turned onto Goat's Hollow Road. "I'm a good listener if you'd like to talk about him."

I shrugged. "There's not much to talk about. I only saw him for a second, and then he was gone."

"What made you think he was related?"

"Didn't you see him?"

"Only briefly. He was on the balcony, and I had my back to him. I didn't notice him until he started to run. He shoved me down before I could react."

I blinked, noticing the bump on his temple and the trace of dried blood. Then I was angry with myself for not noticing it sooner. I reached out and touched his face. "You hit your head."

"It's just a bump. It'll be fine."

He parked in the circular drive in front of the house and stopped the Escalade.

I didn't move. My legs and arms felt too heavy to lift. A single question kept burning its way through my mind. I didn't think I'd be able to think about anything else until I found the answer.

"What is it?" Hal asked gently.

I frowned.

"I'm sure your mom will clear this up. Maybe the guy's just someone who looks like your dad. That happens all the time."

I couldn't tell him I knew at a bone-deep level that I'd met my brother. I couldn't explain it to anyone else because I couldn't explain it to myself.

The question burned another trail across my brain, and I suddenly couldn't stand it. I looked at Hal. "Why was he there?" I asked him. "How is he mixed up in this?"

"I don't know, honey. The best thing to do is to tackle this in manageable bites. Talk to your mom first. We'll take it from there."

I nodded, knowing he was right. Talking to my mom was the logical first step.

So why was I dreading it with every fiber in my body?

I PLOPPED onto the couch and sat with my cell phone in my hand. Nails clicked on the entrance tiles and then disappeared as the pibl's paws hit carpeting. A beat later, a large, golden form leaped onto the couch, and a wet tongue scoured a trail over my exposed knee. Summer was Caphy's favorite time of year. Shorts exposed a lot more flesh for her to kiss.

"Hey, sweet girl."

"Meow!" LaLee yelled. She jumped onto the couch cushion and up onto the back, where she sprawled casually over the top as if she were the queen and the couch was her throne. The diva was apparently peeved that I hadn't been around to hear her laments all morning.

Though I was dreading the call I was about to make, my fur-babies made me feel better. Caphy made me feel loved, and LaLee made me feel needed. After all, every diva needs an audience.

Hal came into the living room and handed me a frosty

glass of lemonade. I thanked him, tears filling my eyes at how lucky I was. "You're all the best."

He kissed the top of my head. "I'll have lunch ready in twenty minutes. I think it's a good time to call Paris right now."

Message received. I needed to bite the bullet and call my mom. Sighing, I found her number in my favorites and tapped it. Caphy sprawled out alongside my leg and fell asleep with a sigh, her squishy head hanging over the front of the couch.

LaLee gave me a running commentary of her morning, punctuated with some tail-whipping and the occasional semi-angry yowl. I interpreted the yowls as her description of how her sister had made her persnickety feline life miserable.

I actually found myself grinning at the thought.

The phone rang several times, and I started to think Joline wasn't going to answer.

Ethel Squeaks trotted into the living room and bumped her snout against my knee, her curly tail whirling happily behind her.

"Hello, pretty piggy." I scratched the thatch of hair between her oversized ears. "Did you get a yummy treat?" In answer, she squealed softly and ran toward the kitchen. I wasn't sure if she was going to get her ball or to beg for more food from Hal. Caphy jumped down and ran after her, no doubt worried she was going to miss out on a treat.

I was so entertained by the squealing and whining sounds coming from the kitchen, I nearly missed the moment when my mother finally answered her phone.

"Joey, honey. This is a surprise."

"Hi mom. I hope I'm not interrupting your dinner."

She gave me a happy little laugh. "Oh no, honey. We won't go out for another few hours."

I winced. It was nearly seven PM in Paris. I couldn't imagine waiting to eat until nine or ten. "How's Garland?"

"He's wonderful." I could hear the love in her voice, and it made me happy. "I'm so glad we made this trip together."

"Are you seeing a lot of the sights?"

"We are. He's in meetings for several hours a day. But I make good use of my time."

"That's good."

There was a beat of silence as my mother read between the lines and into my forced cheerfulness. "What's wrong, Joey?"

"What makes you think something's wrong?" I said, knowing it was a weak deflection.

"I know you. I can tell when you're upset about something. I presume you called because you wanted to talk to me about it...whatever it is. So, talk to me."

"I don't know how to start."

"Just spit it out." Joline's voice was filled with worry, almost as if she knew what I was going to ask.

I hesitated another beat and then sighed. "Mom, I need to ask you something, and I need you to be honest with me."

"Of course, honey..."

"No, I mean it. Totally honest. This affects more than just me."

Silence met my words. I could almost feel my mom bristling through the phone line. "Do you think I lie to you on a regular basis?"

I bit back a quick response, knowing it wouldn't go well. She'd lied to me about a lot of stuff over the years. Most of it life-changing. "I'm not accusing you of anything, Mom. I just want to know the truth."

"Just. Ask. Me."

"Do I have a brother?"

If silence had a texture, hers would be like porcupine quills. For several seconds, I sat and waited for her to answer, not knowing what to expect. Was she just stunned by the question? Or was she trying to come up with an expedient lie that I'd believe?

Finally, I couldn't take it anymore. "Mom?"

She made a small noise that sounded like a terrified mouse.

"Mom, talk to me."

"Oh Joey."

Heat flared in my cheeks, and pretty little stars burst before my eyes. "I do, don't I?"

"He. Oh, honey..."

"Where has he been, mom? Why didn't you tell me?" Anger sizzled along my spine, making me feel like a rocket preparing to erupt.

"I never expected your paths to cross. They weren't supposed to..." A small sob broke the tension on the line. "He wasn't supposed to know."

"Please speak to me in full, coherent sentences, mom. Or I swear I'm going to lose it."

She sucked air and went silent for a beat. Then, finally, "His name is Joshua. Aside from you, he was the most beautiful baby in the world."

Tears slid down my cheeks. I knew she was crying too because the tears clogged her voice.

"We were so young. Too young to be parents. And your father had such big plans. But we just couldn't..." She swallowed audibly. "We gave him up, Joey. We did it because we loved him. But we told the adoption people not to tell him about us. We didn't think we'd be able to stay away if he knew about us." She sniffled loudly. "Oh, honey. I'm sorry. We tried to ensure this wouldn't happen."

Reality crashed down on me, pressing me into the couch. I felt as if I weighed a thousand pounds. The phone suddenly felt too heavy to hold. "I have a brother."

"Yes, Joey. You have a brother. I had him during my junior year in college. And giving him up was the hardest thing I've ever done."

15

———

"But why?" I asked my mother.

"Why what?" She was crying. Her voice was thick with tears.

"Why didn't you ever tell me? I could have gotten to know him. We could have been friends."

"That's exactly what we didn't want!" my mother yelled, shocking us both. She sniffed and sighed. "I'm sorry. This is hitting me harder than I would have expected. Honey, Joshua was part of our past. We had to leave him there."

"But why?" I asked, my own tears making it hard to talk.

There was a moment of silence, thick with tension. When she spoke again, I could barely hear her. "You have no idea what it took out of me...of us...to walk away from that baby. He was a symbol of the love your father and I shared. He was part of *us*. But it would have been unfair to try to keep him. We were too young, and our lives were still unfolding."

"Unfair to whom?" I asked, suddenly so angry. "To you? It wasn't Joshua's fault you had him. You should have stepped up. You should have..."

"Unless you've been faced with the same situation," my mother barked. "Don't you dare judge me."

I knew she was right. I did. Deep down. But I was overwhelmed by such a feeling of loss. I could have had a brother.

"The people who took him have loved him and cared for him as we would have never been able to," Joline said. "They've been grateful every day to have him in their lives."

It took me a moment to understand what her words meant. "You've kept up with them?"

"We have." There was a smile in her voice. "I know everything about his life. Schools, awards, sports..."

"So he knew he was adopted?" I interrupted.

Silence.

"Mom?"

"We didn't want him to know. We didn't want anything to keep him from being the happiest he could be."

I wasn't sure how I felt about that, so I didn't comment. Instead, I said, "I need to speak to his adopted parents."

"No, Joey."

"You don't understand, Mom. I *need* to talk to them."

"Joey, this isn't about you or what you need. Joshua has a right to live his own life."

"No, Mom. He doesn't. Not anymore."

"What are you talking about?" There was a beat of silence and then, "How did you find out about him?" Her tone was suspicious.

"He's here. In Deer Hollow. And I'm afraid he's mixed up in something really bad. I need to speak to him, but he's hiding from me. So I have to talk to his parents. I need their help to reach him."

"I don't have the right to give you their number," she

argued. "The Magness's have requested we not tell family members who they are. They were very insistent on that."

All the blood ran from my face and ice filled my chest. I knew that name. And, suddenly, I knew why my brother had shown up in Deer Hollow. "Do the Magness's have any other children?" I asked.

"Joey..."

"Answer me!" I screamed. "Joshua has shown up in the middle of a murder investigation. I need to get ahead of this. I need to know why he's here and what he has to do with all of it."

"Murder?" A soft sob slid through the phone. "No. That's not possible."

"I'd love to agree with you," I told her. "If that's true, Hal and I will do everything we can to protect him. But I need more information. I need to know what he knows. And why he's here."

My pleas finally got through to her. In a voice that was little more than a whisper, she said, "They have a daughter. Her name is Karinne."

My world shrank down to a pinprick of light as dizziness swamped me.

"Give me their phone number," I demanded.

"No. Even if Josh is involved in something bad, the Magness's have a right to their privacy."

"Jeezopete, Mother!"

"Give me a couple of hours. Let me speak to them. I'll get back to you." Without further warning, she was gone.

I turned to Hal. He was sitting next to me on the couch, the pibl snoring softly between us. I could tell by the expression on his handsome face that he understood the situation from my side of the conversation. "I'm so sorry, honey."

I nodded, scrubbing at my wet cheeks and sniffling. "We need to find him."

"Yes," he said. "We do. But only after you have something to eat. When you talk to your brother, you want to be calm and reasonable. Maybe he has a perfectly understandable reason for being at both scenes."

I felt the corners of my lips curving upward, partly because Hal was in my corner and partly because he assumed that in my current state, I could locate *reasonable* in a tiny room, using both hands and with a flashlight hat on my head.

"Are you implying I won't be calm if I don't eat?"

He arched a midnight brow at me. "Next to the word, Hangry, in the dictionary is your beautiful face."

I gave him a watery laugh. "Okay. I'll eat. But only if you'll perform your PI magic and find out everything you can about the Magness's, including Karinne and my brother Joshua."

He leaned in and kissed my forehead. "It would be my pleasure."

I climbed to my feet, feeling a hundred years old, and headed upstairs to wash my face.

THE TEXT from my mother came as we were finishing up a late lunch. She'd come through with a phone number for the Magness's. Despite that, I wasn't enthused about calling them. My mom's rationale for protecting their privacy must have sunk in, making guilt a factor in my decision-making process.

Still, if Joshua was in trouble, his adoptive parents might want to have a chance to help.

Despite my reservations, I was disappointed when they didn't answer the phone.

"I'll do a reverse search on the number," Hal said. "It's a three one seven number, so it's probably in Indianapolis."

He was almost right. It turned out the Magness's lived in Nineveh, Indiana. A small lake community about twenty-five minutes from Deer Hollow. Hal looked up from jotting down the address. "Do you feel like taking a drive?"

"I do. Let's take Caphy, though. She's been cooped up all day."

JOSHUA AND KARINNE'S parents lived in a two-story, cabin-style home overlooking a large pond with a fountain in the center. The trees clung closely to the winding gravel drive, making me think for a few minutes that we'd taken a wrong turn.

When the house came into view a moment later, I was charmed.

A taupe color with burgundy doors and large windows, the home was adorned on three sides with a wide balcony and had a backdrop of dense woods behind it. The steeply sloping lawn was lush and green, with flowers planted in a raised bed built of railroad ties at the corner closest to the drive.

A profusion of brightly-hued flowers overflowed several pots on the deck and front porch, as well as in boxes arrayed along the wide railing.

When we pulled up to the house, a man came out of the matching detached garage, an elderly red dachshund ambling along near his feet. Inside the garage, the hood of a large, silver truck was open, and a radio played rock music from the nineties.

The man watched us climb out of Hal's car, his wary gaze sliding from us to a barking Caphy in the back seat. "Don't let that dog out of your car, now," the man said with heat in his voice. "Gus here's afraid of big dogs."

"No worries, sir," Hal said. "It's nice and shady here, and the windows are cracked. She can stay in the car."

I nodded in agreement. Though Caphy would have loved to go for a run on the property, it was Gus's home, and he deserved to feel safe.

Besides, the pibl would probably dive into the pond. She'd smell like wet dog and fish all the way home and need a bath.

Hal offered his hand to the homeowner. "Mr. Magness?"

The man didn't take Hal's hand. His eyes narrowed suspiciously. "We don't take to solicitors here. This is a private neighborhood, and that's the way we like it."

Hal pulled out his credentials and showed them to the homeowner. "I'm sorry to bother you. I'm a private investigator working with the Deer Hollow police."

A woman came outside, her dark eyes cold and her body language closed. She had a dishtowel thrown over one shoulder, and her face was moist as if she'd been doing something strenuous when we'd arrived. Mrs. Magness's hair was the same color as Karinne's, and she wore it in a riot of curls around her square face. She slid a look toward the car, and her gaze softened when she saw my pibl's squishy face sticking out of the window.

Caphy reacted by whining softly, her whole backend wagging in a frenzied greeting.

"That your dog?" Mrs. Magness asked me.

I nodded. "That's Caphy. She's very friendly."

"It's a Pitbull, Zoie. Keep your distance." Apparently, old Gus wasn't the only male in the family who didn't like big dogs.

Mrs. Magness blew air through her lips. "Just because she's a pitty doesn't make her mean, JD."

I smiled at the woman, liking her. "She doesn't have a mean bone in her body. But I understand the hesitation. They're intimidating."

"Why are you here?" Mr. Magness asked. He crossed his arms over his chest and glared at me as if I'd shouted an obscenity.

"It's about Karinne," Hal said. "And Joshua."

Both Magness's paled, their gazes meeting and flashing with some kind of silent message. Mrs. Magness's gaze slid to the house as if she were contemplating making a run for it.

"What about them?" JD asked, clearly not liking that we were there, upsetting his world.

"I'm sure you heard about the murders in Deer Hollow?" Hal asked gently.

JD's face turned red. His oil-painted hands fisted. "Our kids didn't have anything to do with those murders. How dare you come here and accuse them? Get off our property!"

"JD," his wife soothed.

"No!" He stepped toward Hal as if intending to attack. "I want you both off my property right now."

"We aren't accusing them of murder, sir," Hal said. "We just need to question your son on his whereabouts. He's a person of interest. Wouldn't you like him to have a chance to clear himself?"

JD Magness stabbed a finger at the truck. Caphy whined and barked, throwing herself at the door as she reacted to the man's aggression.

In response, little Gus started barking too, his voice surprisingly deep for such a small dog.

Magness noticed Caphy's agitation. "I'll go get my gun and shoot that dog if she gets out of that car."

"JD!" Mrs. Magness barked at her husband. "Shut your mouth and calm down."

The door to the house opened and slammed shut behind a familiar figure. "It's okay, Dad."

We all turned as Karinne descended the two steps to the driveway. "I'll talk to them."

"No, Rinnie," JD said, taking a step toward his daughter.

"I want to. Please. Can you take Gus inside and give us some privacy?"

The Magness's stared at their daughter for a moment, clearly reluctant to leave her with us. But after some encouragement from his wife, JD Magness finally relented, scooping up old Gus and following his wife into the house.

Karinne looked at me and nodded toward the truck. "Can she come out and play? I've always wanted a pitty, and she seems really sweet."

"I don't think that's a good idea," I told her.

Karinne's eyes filled with tears. She sniffed and scrubbed at them. "I'm sorry. I'm just a little emotional right now. Really, it's okay. If my dad gets upset, I'll tell him I made you do it."

I hesitated.

"Please?" She looked down at the ground. "To tell you the truth, I need an emotional support animal right now. I lost my dog when my husband and I split, and I miss her."

I nodded at Hal, and he went to let Caphy out. Before letting her loose, he clipped a leash on her, then led her to Karinne.

The pibl was so excited her whole body was wagging.

The moment she swiped a big kiss over Karinne's arm, the other woman was on her knees, her arms wrapped around my dog.

It nearly broke my heart. Something was clearly going on with her.

My softhearted PI handed Karinne his clean handkerchief. She took it and gave him a watery smile. "Thanks. Why don't we walk down to the pond?"

I nearly grimaced. Caphy would surely be in the water if I let her. "Okay, but we'll need to keep hold of the leash, or you're going to have a pibl-shaped fish in your pond."

Karinne laughed, pushing to her feet.

We walked for a moment in silence, allowing Karinne to regain her equilibrium. By the time we sat down on the bench overlooking the fountain, she seemed calm again. Caphy lay down on the grass and dropped her head onto her paws, watching the fountain as if she wanted to play with it. I had no doubt she did.

"In my senior year of high school, I was filled with a desire to change the world. Not so different from all my friends, but unlike them, I found an outlet for it. A friend of mine urged me to come with her to intern for an Indianapolis city council candidate, and I thought that would be fun. It *was* fun at first. Exciting. Especially since the candidate was so charming." She winced. "At least, he seemed that way to me. I was young and stupid." She toed off her flip-flops and rubbed her bare foot over Caphy's soft back. My dog turned her head and licked Karinne's toes in thanks.

Karinne giggled. "She's awesome."

"She is."

"I'm sorry my dad was such a jerk about her."

"No worries. People have a right to their opinions." I fell silent, wanting her to get back to her story. I heard a soft splash and turned in time to see a rock skip several times over the lake's surface. Hal had moved away to give Karinne privacy with her story. He could no doubt tell what was coming.

Unfortunately, so could I.

Karinne sighed. "It started with small things. Fingers brushing and lingering a bit longer than they should. Then a hand on the back that did the same. But then he started encouraging me to join him at the diner across the street to work. And then, we were alone in the office one night..."

I reached out and grabbed her hand, squeezing it. "Did he hurt you?"

She shook her head, sniffling. "He was inappropriate. He made me really uncomfortable, but he didn't rape me. I thought I could control the behavior at first. I tried to keep at least one other person with us at all times. But he was a master manipulator, and he was good at maneuvering me into delicate situations." She frowned. "My friend didn't believe he was giving me unwelcome attention. She accused me of trying to seduce him. I think she was jealous."

My heart broke a little for the eighteen-year-old girl who'd had to deal with a jerk of an adult who should have known better.

"The worst part is," she glanced at me, tears shimmering in her gaze. "He liked to keep trophies."

My stomach twisted. "He kept something of yours?"

She shuddered violently. When she spoke, her voice sounded slightly strangled, almost too soft to hear. "Yes."

I wrapped an arm around her shoulders and tugged her close. "I'm so sorry you went through that."

Sniffling, she nodded. "When I threatened to tell, Martin Robb promised to ruin my family. He had lots of friends in government and business. I knew he'd do it. So I just stopped coming into the office. I begged my parents to let me go visit my aunt in New York for the rest of the summer."

"And he left you alone?"

She nodded. "Unfortunately, Joshua found out what happened."

"How?"

"My..." She made air quotes with her fingers. "Friend told him."

Women could be such skunks. "What did he do?"

She glanced at me. "Nothing overt. He knew how dangerous getting on Robb's bad side could be. But Josh is really smart, and he's dedicated himself to getting information on Robb. He's been working on finding the right kind of proof to sink him for years."

That kind of tenacity was both admirable and a little scary, I thought. Then a wave of sadness slid through me. I had a brother. And he was smart and determined. I thought I'd probably like him if we ever met.

"When I found out the client whose party we were catering was Robb, I panicked. I called Josh and asked him what I should do. I wanted to just walk away. But I really need this job. I need to get my own place so I can have Daisy again."

"Daisy?"

She smiled. "My dog. She's a lab mix. Really sweet like Caphy. But my dad's afraid of big dogs, so I can't have her here."

There was a twinkle in her eye, so I tweaked her a little. "I thought Old Gus was the one who was afraid of big dogs?"

She snorted out a laugh. "I'm afraid dad's using Gus as an excuse. Truth is, Dad was attacked by a dog once. It happened to be a Rottweiler. But Dad was only five, and the attack has stuck with him." She gave me a sad smile. "He loves that crotchety little dachshund. I don't want to burst his bubble by telling him a little dog's far more likely to bite than a big one."

I chuckled, not sure that was precisely true, but knowing people tended to underestimate the ferocity of a yapper and overestimate the ferociousness of a large breed. "Anybody who loves a dog is my people," I told her with a smile.

Her eyes glossy with unshed tears, she nodded.

"Was that encounter when you were eighteen what Robb was talking to you about at the ice cream place?"

She shrugged. "Partly. Not really. He just reminded me I had a lot to lose if I told anybody about that."

Some instinct told me that wasn't all there was to it. "What else?"

She turned to me, her gaze sharpening. Then she sighed. "He accused me of trying to blackmail him."

"Robb was being blackmailed?"

"Apparently. He seemed to be casting around to figure out who it was."

My thoughts returned to Benson Dexter claiming he was being blackmailed. He'd assumed it was Wickham and Calliente. Could he have been right?

After a moment's hesitation, Karinne said, "You're wrong about Josh."

I bit back a denial that I thought my...our...brother killed Pam Wickham. "Tell me why he's been all over this thing. I promise I have an open mind."

She sighed. "He's like a dog with a bone. He refuses to let go of this Robb thing." Rather than anger, I saw pride in her eyes when she turned to me. "He's determined to bring him down."

I chose my words carefully, knowing how they'd sound.

"Setting Robb up on two murders and one attempted murder would definitely bring him down."

She blinked in surprise. "Two murders?"

I nodded. "Mr. Calliente's fiancé, Pam, was also killed. M...your brother was at the scene."

Her eyes went wide. "Josh was there when she was murdered?"

"I'm not sure about that, but when we went back after the police were done, he was in the victim's apartment."

She deflated a little, looking strangely relieved. "That actually makes perfect sense. Josh believed Calliente was blackmailing Robb for business. Calliente Catering recently acquired several powerful new clients, all friends of Mayor Robb's. When I told Josh that Robb and Jonathan were like oil and water, he decided blackmail had to be involved."

"What would Calliente have had to blackmail Robb with?"

She chewed her bottom lip. "People have speculated that Robb's trademark..." she made air finger quotes, "charm, might have gotten him into trouble."

"Sexual misconduct?"

She shrugged.

"And you believe that's why Robb and Calliente didn't get along?"

"Why else?"

"I've heard speculation that Calliente overcharged the mayor for the catering services."

"Oh yeah, he definitely did that. But that's the cart, not the horse."

I frowned, not understanding.

"Jonathan only kicked up his prices after we got the slew of new clients." She shook her head. "Love him or hate him, Jonathan Calliente was a good businessman. If what I suspect is true, he forced Robb to recommend him to a who's-who of powerful acquaintances and then upped the ante by charging all of them too much for his services. Sounds like a win-win scenario for Jonathan's business."

Funny, it sounded like motive to me. "Karinne, we need to talk to your brother. Do you know where he is?"

She shook her head, a mulish glint in her eyes.

"If he's innocent, he'll want to give his side of the story."

Karinne's already hard gaze turned brittle. "Josh didn't kill anybody."

"If that's true, he shouldn't mind coming forward." When she didn't respond, I said, "He's been seen at two of the three crime scenes. He really needs to come in and clear his name."

Something in my tone must have gotten through to her. "I really don't know where he is. He hasn't been home for a few days. I assumed he was staying in Deer Hollow."

Thinking of my brief conversation with Lis about contacting Karinne's husband, I asked, "Could he be staying with your ex?"

Karinne looked shocked. "David?" She shook her head. "Josh hated David. He wouldn't trust him to have his back on anything. Besides," she said. "My ex took a job in Chicago. I haven't seen or spoken to him in months."

Well, that certainly appeared to be a dead end.

16

I covered my nose and glanced toward the back seat, where a blissfully happy and disturbingly stinky Caphy lay panting. She wagged her tail when she saw me looking at her.

"Bath for you when we get home, girlfriend."

Her wag sagged a bit at the "b" word.

"Ugh!" I groaned. "What was in that lake?"

Hal slid me a grin. "She spent a lot of time in the muck at the edge. You probably don't want to know what was in that."

He wasn't wrong. "So, what do you think about what Karinne told us?"

His smile disappeared. "I wish she'd told us where Joshua was."

"Yeah," I sighed. "Me too. But if it makes you feel any better, I believe her. I don't think she knows where he is."

"It doesn't," he said, glancing my way. "Make me feel any better. I'll admit, I'm not comfortable with the familial connection to you. I can't shake the feeling that you're going to be pulled into this mess somehow."

I stared out the window, my emotions in a whirl. I was torn over whether I wanted to find my brother. On the one hand, I was dying to get to know him. On the other, if we located Joshua Magness, he might end up in jail.

Still, one thing kept popping up in my brain. "Can we go over what we know?" I asked Hal. "I'm having trouble putting *any* of the pieces together."

He nodded. "That's a good idea. This investigation basically has two tracks. The first track would be that someone had a grudge against Calliente and/or his company. That actually makes the most sense because our three victims were all tied to Calliente Catering. But we don't have any strong suspects who have means as well as motive. I've talked to all of Calliente's recent clients by phone, and they all either had strong alibis or weak motives. I'm keeping an eye on a couple of them, but I really don't think there's anything there."

"What about employees?"

"Nothing I've been able to uncover so far. Pam Wickham did send me the employee list before she was killed, and I've done backgrounds on all of them. Some of them were on other jobs in other cities. One was having a baby. A couple were on vacation. The crew at Robb's party consisted of six people. Prince and Karinne are on our radar. The other four were in the yard the entire time until after their boss was killed. They have alibis for the other two attacks."

"Robb might have had motive if what Cecily and Benson told us was true."

"Unfortunately, we didn't recover any blackmailable information with Calliente's body or anywhere else Robb allowed us to search." He frowned. "The reality is that we can't do a thorough search of Robb's office because he's using his connection with Sheriff Mulhern to keep us away. I won't deny that's frustrating."

I nodded. "As far as we know, my brother didn't have means or motive for Calliente's death."

"Right," Hal agreed. "Which brings us to the second investigative track. Robb. We have several people who might have reason to want the mayor dead, including Karinne and Joshua."

"Or Karinne's dad," I offered.

"Right. But since Robb wasn't the victim, I'm having trouble making that case."

"You mentioned that all the victims were connected to Calliente's company, but the same could be said about Robb too. They were all involved in some way with his party."

Hal accelerated onto the highway. The first sign we passed listed Deer Hollow and a few other small towns along the way. We were twenty miles from home. The thought made me happy. I was tired. And worried. And a little sad.

"The strongest possibility for a case against Robb is blackmail. If someone tried to blackmail him, I could see him committing murder," Hal said.

"I could too. But it seems unlikely that three people were in on a blackmail scheme. Wickham and Calliente, definitely. That fits with both Karinne's and Cecily's stories. But how would Prince be involved? Unless he was blackmailing the blackmailers, which takes us to a whole new level of implausible."

"He might have found evidence himself," Hal offered. "Or been in the wrong place at the wrong time."

Talking about Prince reminded me. "How's he doing? Have you heard from Arno about his condition?"

"Arno texted me about it this morning. He's in an

induced coma, The swelling in his brain is still worrisome, but his vitals are apparently strong."

"If he wakes up, he can tell us who beat him."

Hal didn't respond. I knew from the look on his face that the idea didn't make him happy.

"What?"

"He could be in that coma for a few days. I need answers sooner rather than later."

We drove in morose silence for a few minutes. I finally broke it, mostly because I didn't like seeing him so worried. Maybe continuing to shape the case in front of us would drag him out of his funk. "Okay, let's talk fringe players."

He straightened in his seat, his chin coming up a fraction of an inch. "Okay."

"Cecily and Benson," I said. "Cecily dislikes Robb, but I don't see that she has much of a motive for murder. Agree?"

"He did have something to do with Katherine Leonard's death. Not directly, maybe, but his underhanded dealings led to her being murdered. That's a pretty good motive."

He was right. Cecily and Katherine had been lifelong friends. "Okay, right. I'd forgotten about that. So Cecily has motive. Means?"

"She was in Robb's house about the time Calliente was killed. And she was seen fighting with him earlier in the day."

"She could have used a knife to kill him. We have only her word that she didn't." The idea didn't make me happy. I liked Cecily.

"Benson hates Robb. It sounds like he was also being blackmailed by Calliente. He might have thought leaving a body in Robb's kitchen was a good way to take care of both problems."

"But nobody saw him there, right? He wasn't at the party," I said.

"Right. But that doesn't mean he didn't do it. The front door of the house was left unlocked to allow guests to enter. And everyone was in the back yard. So, if someone had come into the house through the front, it's plausible he or she wouldn't have been seen."

"That means the killer could have been anybody."

He frowned. "I'm afraid so."

I let that simmer in my brain for a bit. "Okay, as if this isn't confusing enough..." I grinned at him, and I was happy to see some of the unease lift away as he smiled back. "We have the beautiful new donor who Robb knew a long time ago and wants to know again. On the surface, she seems much too nice to either date Robb or kill two people. She definitely doesn't seem likely to have shot Prince."

"She might have a grudge against Robb for something he did to her in the past," Hal said. "But that wouldn't give her a reason to kill Calliente or his fiancée."

"We just keep coming back to the same problem, don't we?"

"We do."

Hal reached over and clasped my hand, squeezing it before settling our joined hands onto his thigh. "We're forgetting something," I murmured. "I just know there's a detail that makes this all make sense. But I can't quite get a grip on it."

"In my world, that's called a Monday," Hal said, sighing.

My cell rang as I was climbing out of the car at home. Caphy ran toward the pond barking, and I looked at Hal. "It's my mom. Can you get the beast into the laundry room for me? After she eats, I'll hose her off."

"Sure," he said, already heading across the yard.

I hit answer as I glanced toward the pond. Our new family of ducks was trying to enjoy a swim without being harangued by eighty pounds of barking canine. Hal was going to have his hands full pulling the pibl away from such wonderful entertainment.

"Hey, mom."

"Joey, honey. Are you okay?"

I knew what she was asking. Had I come to terms with having a sibling and finding out that my mother had lied to me all my life. She'd actually lied to me about a lot of stuff. I was kind of used to it. But I guessed that wasn't a good thing. "I'm fine."

There was a beat of silence while she probably tried to figure out if I was mad based on my two-word response. "Good. I...um..." She expelled air. "I'm really sorry we didn't tell you, Joey. We thought it would be easier if you didn't know he was out there."

I wasn't in the brain space to talk about how wrong that reasoning was. I almost said as much, but then I decided I didn't want to back away from it. "So, you thought it would be easier to find out that the brother I'd always wished I'd had growing up was living with a different sister?"

"Joey..."

"You thought it would be better for me not to know that he was a good, loyal person who'd go to extraordinary lengths to protect those he loved?"

"Honey, I..."

"You believed that it was a good idea to punish both him and me because you and dad couldn't face the responsibility of raising a child?"

"That's going too far, Joey!"

Yeah, I knew that. But once begun, I couldn't seem to stop myself. My world felt upside down. Everything I'd lived through seemed to have been tainted somehow. "I thought your lies were behind us. I didn't think you could upend my life again. Jeez, I was stupid."

Silence pulsed between us as I gulped air into lungs that suddenly seemed too depleted. I pictured her sitting primly on her side of the call, her pretty face set in that stern expression that had always turned my blood to ice when I was a kid.

When she finally spoke again, I was shocked by her words. "Joshua was a decent student in school. He was capable of more than he achieved, but studies bored him. With one exception. He excelled at math and loved it, even tutoring kids who weren't good at math."

Unbelievably, I heard a smile in her voice. I sat down on the porch stairs, intrigued.

"He's good at every sport he's ever tried but prefers soccer to football. He's quick to temper when he thinks someone has been wronged. And slow to forgive if he's gotten his feelings hurt. He loves to climb. He goes to a climbing wall several times a week and plans to do a real climb in the Rockies one day. He's been saving money for that adventure for two years."

She sniffed, and I realized that somewhere along the line, her smile had turned to tears.

"He's quick and agile and has a big heart." She took a long, shaky breath. "And I've regretted not joining him in his life's adventures every moment of every day since we let him go."

Tears slid down my cheeks as my heart quietly broke into pieces. But it was her muffled sob that really did me in. "I'm so sorry, Mom. I didn't mean what I said. I was just being a brat."

"No, you have a right to be mad. I understand. Believe

me, there have been lots of times that I've been mad at myself. I've missed having him in my life, Joey. That doesn't mean your dad and I have loved you any less. It just means I realize now, as an adult, what I gave up when I was too young to make a decision that big."

"You made the right decision for you and dad. And probably for Josh too," I admitted. "I know that. But," I wasn't sure how to explain to her that I was so jealous of Karinne Magness for getting to grow up with the brother I'd always wanted. "I'm just wishing I could have known him."

She sniffed loudly. "It's not too late," she told me. "I spoke to the Magness's a few minutes ago, honey. I told them we were going to tell Joshua who we are. I want him in our lives. I know it won't be easy. And I feel so bad your dad won't be here to meet the wonderful man our son turned out to be. But it's the right thing to do. I feel that in my heart."

"And Garland?" I fought hope, tempering it with the fact that Joshua was currently a person of interest in a murder investigation.

"He and I have talked about it. He's fully on board. He'll support us in whatever we want."

He would. If I knew anything at all about Garland Medford, it was that he loved my mom more than anything in his life. He'd lasso the moon and give it to her if she wanted him to.

"Good." I took the tissue Hal handed me, smiling my thanks. "When are you coming home?"

"Two days. Garland has a few things to wrap up. We'll leave as soon as we can."

"I might see him before you get here," I warned. "We need to talk to him about the stuff that's been going on." It was weak, but I didn't want her to know how deeply he was immersed in at least one murder. Maybe two.

"I understand. Just..." She hesitated. She wanted to ask me not to turn Josh against her but was afraid the request might hurt my feelings.

"I won't tell him anything about you or your decision. That's between the two of you. I just want to meet him." The thought made my stomach twist with excitement. I squelched it immediately. That way lay potential heartbreak.

"Thanks, honey."

"I'll see you in a couple of days, mom."

"See you soon."

I disconnected and sat staring into space, feeling overwhelmed and suddenly exhausted.

"Everything okay?" Hal asked, sitting down beside me.

"Everything is..." I hesitated to say the word for fear it would turn to ash. "Okay," I finally said. "Everything is okay. Mom wants to tell Josh about us." I turned to my PI, a sense of wonder finding its way into my mind before I could stop it. "I'm going to meet my brother."

He pulled me into a hug. "That's great news, honey."

I nodded, scrubbing at a fresh fall of tears. I knew what he was thinking. I was thinking the exact same thing. But my head couldn't seem to overrule my heart. And I was happy about meeting Josh.

I only hoped he'd be happy to find out about me.

17

Hal's phone rang as we were fixing bowls for Ethel Squeaks and Caphy that evening. "It's Arno," he said, hitting speaker. "Hey, Arno. You're on with Joey and me."

"Good. Then I'll only have to say this once. Officially, I'm supposed to tell you two to butt out of this investigation."

I glanced at Hal, and he arched a midnight brow. "And unofficially?" he asked Arno.

"Unofficially, I wanted to warn you that we found that white car you spotted at the Prince scene. Registration said it belongs to Karinne Magness. It was off the side of the road hidden in some trees out your way."

"On Goat's Hollow?" I asked, alarmed.

"No, on Possum Park Road."

"I know you two talked to Magness in Nineveh. But I sent Schmidt to pick her up, and she wasn't at her parent's home. Any idea where she might have gone?"

"No," Hal said, giving me a questioning look.

I shook my head. Hal probably wondered if he might have missed something when he was giving Karinne her privacy. He hadn't. Not anything that would help Arno find her, anyway.

"There's something else," Arno said.

I refocused my full attention on the cop.

"We found a can of black spray paint in the car. It matches what was sprayed on the cameras at Pam Wickham's murder scene."

Well, dang it and the horse it rode in on.

Hal sighed. "Do you want us to go talk to her parents again? She might have told them where she was going."

"Unlikely," Arno said. "And I don't think that's a good idea. Mulhern heard you were talking to them and had piglets. Maybe you could concentrate on finding the kid you saw at the scene?"

I winced. Even though I'd been anxious to meet my brother, finding him to turn over to the police was way down on the list of things I wanted to do. As in falling off the bottom.

"What about the mayor?" I asked. "Is anybody watching him?"

"I've got that handled. And that's the last place you two want to be."

He wasn't wrong. Still...

Hal left an hour later, after helping me bathe the pibl with the hose. He said he had a lot of computer work to do in an attempt to locate my brother. I sat on the front porch swing and watched as he and Ethel drove away, smiling at the big twitchy ears I could see above the dashboard as he backed around.

Ethel's ears...not Hal's.

Caphy did happy zoomies around the yard for a few minutes. She rolled enthusiastically in the grass, trying to defile her freshly washed fur and generally acting like her normal, happy self.

I shoved against the porch floor with my toes, keeping the swing in a gentle back and forth motion that soothed my jangled nerves. After a few moments, I settled into the pleasure of the warm evening, with the comforting sounds of the bullfrog in the pond and the crickets in the woods. High above me, a veritable explosion of stars turned the night sky into a stunning display of lights.

I laid my head back on the swing and sighed, feeling my nerves settle for the first time all day. I knew I should go inside and finish cleaning up the kitchen, but I was suddenly too tired to move.

At some point, my eyes drifted closed. I dozed, dreaming of warm summer nights chasing fireflies with a jar and counting stars from a blanket spread over the grass. Memories as bright as yesterday brought my childhood back to me in three-dimensional space and color. My bare feet, grass-stained from hours playing in the yard without shoes, danced across the cool grass as my jar lit with magical golden light. In the dream, my cheeks were hot from a day in the sun and my legs itched from an array of mosquito bites. My eyes were bright with the delight of the chase, my lips curved in a perpetual smile.

Happy. I'd been loved and happy. An idyllic childhood.

I was jolted awake by an insistent yowl and a fur-padded blow to my shin. I lifted my head and looked at LaLee. She was heading for the railing, her tail snapping behind her.

"Hello to you too, Diva."

The cat gave me a disgusted look and leaped effortlessly to the wide railing, settling herself into position to watch her crazy sister chase lightning bugs and roll in the grass.

I smiled. "She's a little weird, but she's all ours."

LaLee meowed her agreement.

We sat in comfortable silence for a while. The warmth of my dream clung to me, leaving behind a residual smile I had no will to banish from my face. I was nearly drowsing off again when Caphy started to bark. Taking off toward the pond.

I went on full alert, worried about coyotes. "Caphy! Come back here, girl."

The dog ignored me, of course, and that's when I saw why she'd taken off. I jumped from the swing and started running. "No! No, Caphy! Bad girl."

Waddling leisurely across the grass toward the pond, the mama duck started moving faster when she spotted the pitty running her way. Her downy brown ducklings took her cue and scurried after her.

"Caphy!" I yelled again, cutting the distance between us. But not fast enough.

Caphy was going to overtake the little family before I could get to her.

"No, no, no, no!" Panic flared in my chest, making it hard to breathe.

I dug in, running faster, knowing I wouldn't make it in time.

Then the strangest thing happened. Caphy was within five feet of the ducklings when she screeched to a halt and dropped to her haunches, cocking her head as they toddled toward the pond. Her tail wagged once, and she dropped to her belly, putting her head on her paws to watch them go.

Relief made it possible for me to draw a breath again. Well, that, and the fact that I'd stopped running. Judging by the hoarse sawing of breath through my airways, I needed to get into shape. Caphy and I needed to get back to our daily runs.

"Good girl," I said, relieved when the last baby plunked into the glossy black water and glided away. "Come on, Caphy," I called. When she didn't come, I added, "Time for treats."

She leaped to her feet and flew back toward the house, ignoring me completely in her fervor for a snack.

Laughing at her antics, I turned and started back.

The tree was one of the largest in my yard, probably several hundred years old, with large roots that sank into the earth and sought the water-drenched soil around the pond. It had massive branches that hung overhead and blocked out the starlight, creating a thicker curtain of shadows that provided good cover for someone trying to sneak up on an unsuspecting passerby.

It never occurred to me I needed to worry about those shadows. Until they moved. A large body rammed into my back, thick arms binding me to an unyielding frame at the throat and waist.

I was so stunned I forgot to fight back for the space of a single heartbeat, and then my legs started to flail, my heels smacking into thick calves and my head crashing back against an iron chest.

The arm around my throat shifted upward and clamped me harder, blocking my screams as hot breath, laced with the smell of stale coffee, scoured my face. The angry words were delivered in a harsh, indecipherable whisper that turned my blood to ice. "Stop fighting me and listen very carefully. If you continue to stick your nose into the murders in Deer Hollow, everyone and everything you love will die. I'll start with that private investigator and end with that new brother you're chasing. Do you understand?"

Shock made me go very still. How could this person know Joshua was my brother?

"Do. You. Understand?" The arms around me tightened, compressing my ribs and threatening to cut off my ability to breathe.

I jerked my head in the affirmative, barely able to move beneath the iron control of those arms.

Sour breath washed over my skin with unwelcome heat. "Don't doubt that I can do what I said." I felt his attention shift toward the house. "It would be a shame to lose that gorgeous dog. I like dogs. I'd hate to have to hurt that one."

Suddenly the pressure around my body was gone, and my legs gave out, plunging me to my knees in the thick, cool grass. I gasped for breath, my entire body vibrating with residual fear. By the time I thought to look around for my attacker, the night was empty and still.

I was alone in the no longer comforting shadows of my once-favorite tree.

Pushing to my feet, I stumbled toward the house. I started at a trembling walk and ended up running, my breathing labored and rough.

LaLee leaped down from the railing and followed me into the house. Her expressive blue gaze locked on me as I quickly shut and locked the door. Unable to think beyond just pulling air into my lungs and releasing it, I leaned against the door as numbing adrenaline eased from my system. Its abandonment left me shaking violently and wobbly on my feet.

I thought about calling Hal, even grabbed my phone, but I ultimately decided against it. He didn't need to come hold my hand. He had work to do to find the killer.

Sudden realization had me gasping for air. My legs softened beneath me, and my back hit the door as I slid to my butt on the cool tile floor.

The killer...

I'd bet everything I owned that I'd just met the killer. And he'd threatened to destroy everyone I loved.

My stomach roiled on the thought and I retched, barely making it to my feet and down the hall before my stomach emptied itself on the heels of that thought.

Somehow, I had another killer dogging me, threatening everybody in my life.

18
_____

Even with Caphy draped over the bed next to me, her squishy head heavy on my chest, I barely slept. Sometime around dawn, my body finally succumbed to exhaustion, and I went under, only to be awakened a mere three hours later by the sound of my phone ringing.

Groaning, I rolled over and ignored it, thinking that whoever it was could call me back at a decent hour.

But it kept ringing.

And ringing.

And ringing.

And... "Jeezopete!" I yelled, jerking upright and flinging a pillow at the jangling cell phone on my nightstand. The pillow missed, of course, and sailed across the room, drawing a playful pibl to it like a pig to truffles. She dove off the bed, tackling the pillow and shaking it until it was dead.

Then she took off out of my room, the sound of whipping cotton accompanying her down the stairs to the first floor.

"Great," I mumbled crankily. "Now my pillow's going to

be beaten into submission and probably eaten." I only hoped she wouldn't take it outside and bury it in the back yard, alongside a veritable graveyard of soup bones and chewies.

The face of the cell told me it was Arno on the phone. My finger stabbed the button and hit the speaker button. "Why are you calling me at the buttcrack of dawn?"

"Good morning to you too, sunshine."

"Grumble, grumble, swear."

Arno chuckled. "I have good news. We caught the guy who was driving the white car. I thought you might want to watch the interview."

I bolted upright, all semblance of weariness fleeing me. "You caught him?"

"Am I speaking Armenian?"

I shoved covers off my legs and launched myself from bed. "I'll be there in fifteen minutes." Then I realized he hadn't mentioned my PI. "What about Hal?"

Arno sighed, the sound filled with the emotions I knew he had to keep buried at the station. "I can't risk having him here. Just in case Mulhern comes in. If the sheriff finds out you two are still working the case, I'll never talk him into reinstating your boyfriend as civilian support."

"He isn't going to be any happier finding me there," I said.

"You and I are planning Lis's surprise birthday party. Shh, don't tell anybody."

"That might work," I agreed.

"It has to."

"Or you might lose your job," I said, knowing Arno wouldn't admit to his fears in that area but also knowing it was a real possibility.

"Don't tease me, Joey. It's not nice."

My lips twitched into a grin. "You're saying you wouldn't mind losing your job?"

"Right at this moment? I'm thinking a beach anywhere might be nice."

I couldn't disagree. "Can I tell Hal that I'm coming?"

"Already handled. See you in twenty-five minutes."

What could I say? My friend sometimes knew me better than I knew myself.

Arno was perched on the corner of Deputy Brian Miller's desk when I was shown into the bullpen. He stood up when I started toward them. His lips were moving, but he wasn't speaking loud enough for me to hear him across the room. I figured he was talking to Miller, but the young cop's attention was on whatever he was doing on the computer.

"Yeah, your girlfriend just came in," Arno said as I reached him. He nodded toward the cell phone on the desk and tapped his lips with his finger.

"Morning, honey," Hal said.

"Hey, handsome." I couldn't help it. Despite everything, I smiled.

"I'm going to assume you were talking to me and not Willager," Hal said, his deep voice playfully stern.

"You know what they say about assuming, Amity," Arno teased.

To me, he said, "I'll be taking my phone into the interview with me. You can watch from the room next door."

I followed Arno to the hall where the interview rooms were located and went through the door he indicated. As I entered the room, my gaze was drawn to the man pacing the room, his gaze occasionally skimming in my direction as if he knew I was watching.

Arno quietly closed the door behind him. "Mr. Magness, please take a seat at the table."

"I'd rather not," the man who looked so much like my dad responded, his manner hostile and belligerent. The squared shoulders and uplifted chin almost made me smile. I had many memories of Brent Fulle doing exactly the same thing when somebody he considered his lesser tried to "instruct" him.

I had some authority issues of my own. A realization that surprised me a bit. I'd always considered myself to be more like my mom. But I'd apparently taken one trait from my dad as well.

"If you'd rather be cuffed to your chair, I can arrange that," Arno said.

Joshua threw another glance toward the mirror on the wall. Nobody was ever fooled into believing it was a mirror. I'd never understood why they even attempted the ruse.

"Who's watching this?" Joshua asked, blue-gray eyes narrowing as he approached the glass.

I flinched back by instinct and then forced myself to move closer, enjoying the first unobstructed view of my brother I'd ever had.

Close up, I could see the freckles sprinkled across his nose and cheeks. The unruly mop of red-brown hair hung nearly into his eyes, and a matching fringe of lashes would have made any woman jealous.

I'd thought him skinny the first time I'd seen him but realized his arms were taut with muscle. Not bulky and thick, but lean and probably just as strong. His lean strength would make him faster, more agile. Just as he'd been described.

Thoughts of my mother's obvious pain when discussing Josh made my chest hurt. What would she think if she saw him standing in an interview room at the sheriff's station?

Joshua's jaw was square, his lips well-shaped and full,

and his nose was strong, just like our dad's had been. He was a very good-looking guy. But there was a hardness in his gaze that made me sad. It spoke of years of mistrust and too-serious pursuits.

While I'd lived my life, surrounded by the security and comfort of a home and friends, he'd spent a lot of his adult life trying to right a single wrong.

Because he loved his sister.

I fought the jolt of quick jealousy that thought engendered.

"Sit down, Mr. Magness." Arno's voice clearly represented his impatience.

With a final glance at the mirror, Joshua turned and dropped into the nearest chair. He had his back to me, which was unfortunate. I'd hoped to watch his expressions as he answered Arno's questions.

Arno sat down across from him, placing his phone on the table. "Now, Mr. Magness, would you like to tell me what you were doing on Goat's Hollow Road last night?"

My heart stopped beating. All the air in my lungs escaped, and stars burst before my eyes. Had he been there? Near my house? When I'd...

The sound emerging from my throat was like the cry of a terrified animal. I hugged myself as ice prickled along my spine. What was happening? Had my brother been the one to threaten me? And why hadn't Arno told me he'd had Joshua in custody last night? Why would my brother want to threaten me?

The stars dancing in front of me turned to dark splotches on the air, and my chest hurt. Realizing I hadn't taken a real breath for a full minute, I opened my mouth and filled my lungs. The spots fell away, but the panic clawing at my throat was still there.

I wasn't going to get the answers to all my questions until Arno completed his interview...if then...so I forced myself to listen.

It was one of the hardest things I'd ever had to do. All I wanted was to crash that interview and demand answers to my questions. Instead, I had to content myself with hearing responses to Arno's inquiries.

"We found your car, Mr. Magness. It looked like you'd tried to hide it. Why would you try to hide your car?" Though Arno's delivery was calm and carefully emotionless, there was no mistaking the steel behind the words. If he'd been speaking with a timid man, he might have had better success getting Josh to open up.

"I have no idea why you think I was hiding it. The car just died. I couldn't get it to start again, so I pushed it off the road. I was just trying to find a phone to call for help when your people dragged me in here."

Arno stared at him for a beat and then inclined his head. "We'll let that ride for now. Please tell me why you were recognized at the scene of an attack on Anthony Prince?"

Joshua leaned back in his chair, arms crossed over his chest. "I don't know who that is."

"Really?" Arno asked pleasantly. "He's a friend of your sister's. I'd think you would have met him at some point."

Josh shrugged. "I don't know all of her friends."

Arno tugged a piece of paper from the folder he'd carried into the room. "Have you seen this gun before?"

I sucked air, slapping a hand over my mouth before realizing the two men couldn't hear me.

Joshua's back tightened. I didn't need to see his face to know the question alarmed him. He shifted slightly in his chair, telescoping nervousness like a deer getting ready to flee a predator. "I've never seen that gun before."

The way Arno stared at him, I got the feeling Josh had just stepped into some kind of trap. "That's surprising. I'm guessing you've never seen this either?" He slid another picture toward my brother. Josh pulled it close and then shoved it away. He glanced toward the camera high in the corner before turning back to Arno. "That's my spray paint. So what?"

Arno's gaze slid to mine for just the briefest second and then dropped back to Josh. "Look, Mr. Magness. Here's the deal." He stabbed a finger on the picture of the gun. "This gun was used in an attack on Anthony Prince. We found it in your car."

"That's not possible!" Joshua surged to his feet so violently, his chair fell over backward with a crash.

I jumped at the sound, my pulse ratcheting up even higher than it already was.

Arno stood too. Placing his hands on the surface of the scarred, wooden table, he leaned in, his manner menacing. "You're lying, Mr. Magness. You've lied about every single thing since we came into this room. When a man lies to me about anything, it makes it much harder for me to believe him about everything else. But when a man lies every time he opens his mouth..."

Arno let that hang between them. Joshua stood absolutely still for a long moment. His back was ramrod straight, and his hands were tightly fisted. Finally, he dipped his chin and sighed. Some of the tension left his back and shoulders, but his hands stayed fisted. When he spoke, his voice was tight. "I had nothing to do with Prince's attack. I have never shot a gun in my life. If he's a friend of my sister's, I hope he's going to be okay." Josh spoke softly, the words seemingly dredged from deep inside his soul.

Arno motioned to the chair. "Please sit."

After a moment's hesitation, Joshua righted his downed chair and sat.

"It's time to tell the truth," Arno said. "You're involved in all these attacks somehow. I need to know how."

Josh stared at the table for a long moment. I took deep breaths and tried to calm the racing of my heart. Fear was a sour taste in my mouth. Fear that he was going to admit to killing Pam Wickham. Fear that he'd shot Prince.

Anxiety crawled through my stomach like a living organism. I pressed my hands against it, trying to breathe through the unsettling sensation.

"I didn't kill anyone," Josh suddenly said, his head snapping up. "I didn't shoot that Prince guy. I'm only trying to get some justice for my sister. And for all the other women who've suffered under Martin Robb."

I blinked in surprise. His admission was unexpected, despite the fact that Karinne had told me pretty much the same thing.

"Why were you at the scene when Prince was attacked?"

He shook his head. "He said something to Karinne. I was going to ask him about it."

"What did he say?" Arno asked.

"He claimed Robb's days of abusing women were coming to an end. He seemed really sure about it. I suspected he might have some evidence."

"So you went inside his hotel room?"

"I never got the chance. When I got there that PI and..." He shook his head. "I left."

"How did the gun get into your car?" Arno asked.

"I told you, I don't know about any gun."

Arno let that hang on the air for a beat and then said. "You were at the scene of Pam Wickham's murder. Were you trying to hide your tracks?"

Josh made a sound like a frustrated growl. "How many times do I have to tell you I didn't kill that woman?"

"Then why were you in her room?"

"I..." He pulled air into his lungs and slowly released it as if he were trying to calm himself. "I think she and the owner of Calliente Catering had something on Robb. I was trying to find it."

Arno leaned closer. "What kind of *something*?"

"Evidence that Martin Robb raped several women. Women who worked for him. Women who couldn't fight back. Women he could frighten or pay off to keep their mouths shut."

My eyes went wide. Our theory about Calliente and Wickham blackmailing Robb was right after all. But how did Prince figure into it?

As if he'd read my mind, Arno asked, "Why would Anthony Prince have been attacked?"

Joshua leaned over the table as if preparing to tell a secret. "He and Pam Wickham were having an affair. I think he found something at Robb's house. Something that would implicate Robb in the rapes. I think he shared that something with her."

Arno's gaze slid toward the mirror where I stood, the action so brief I was surprised Josh caught it. But he did. He turned in the chair, his familiar gaze finding me unerringly through the one-way glass, pinning me to the spot. "Who's watching this?" he asked, his blue-gray eyes narrowing. "Is Robb in there?"

"Nobody's watching," Arno said, his tone dismissive.

Josh turned back to him. "Now who's lying, cop?"

If the accusation made Arno uncomfortable, he gave no indication. "Did you spray paint the cameras at the Fawn Hotel?"

"I did."

"Did you do it so you could kill Pam Wickham?"

Josh just sighed and shook his head.

"Unless you give me a better reason, that's what I'm left with," Arno said.

"I was going to search her room, and I didn't want any video evidence that I'd been in there. I was waiting for her to leave her room so I could search it." His gaze lifted to Arno's. When he spoke again, his voice broke around the edges. "Your boss was there, so I left."

"You went back the next day."

"Yes. I needed to search the place before you clods had a chance to mess with my evidence."

The statement was so outrageous, Arno laughed. "*Your* evidence? Are you aware that cops don't just fall into their jobs by mistake. We have training. Lots of it. What kind of police training have you had, Mr. Magness?"

Josh stared at Arno. I really wished I could see his expression. Judging by Arno's reaction, my brother wasn't bothered in the least by the comparison of his skills to Arno's.

"You're very smug for someone who's about to go to jail," Arno said.

I flinched at that and then realized Arno had said jail, not prison. It was a careful misrepresentation meant to scare my brother. Josh would likely go into a cell for twenty-four hours while Arno tried to make a case against him. But I wasn't sure he'd be convicted with purely circumstantial evidence. The gun in his car was definitely problematic, but it could have easily been planted.

I stopped myself, realizing I'd been trying to justify and make light of things to clear Joshua in my mind. Just because he was my brother by blood, that didn't make him a good person by default. I didn't know him at all, and it would do me good to remember that.

On the other side of the glass, Arno had changed tactics. "The car you've been driving around in belongs to your sister, Karinne, doesn't it?"

Josh's entire posture changed, tightened. "Leave her out of this."

"Sorry, we can't do that. It seems that she might have a better reason than you do to go after Mayor Robb. Maybe she left that gun in the car?"

Joshua was on his feet again, his posture aggressive. Hands fisted, he leaned toward Arno. "You leave her out of this, or I swear..."

"Sit down, Mr. Magness. You're not in control right now. The sooner you figure that out, the better it will go for everyone."

Joshua spun on his heel and took two long strides, his enraged face mere inches from the glass. He stabbed an angry finger at a spot just above my head. "Whoever you are, know this, I have rights. My sister has rights. First of all, she has a right not to be manhandled by entitled jerks with more power than sense. Leave her out of this. She's not the culprit of this mess. She's just a victim." By the time he got to the last sentence, his manner had gone from mutinous to sorrowful.

And I had tears in my eyes. Joshua Magness might never be a real brother to me. He might have killed someone and tried to kill others. But, when I was growing up, I'd have given almost anything for a brother who'd stand up for me like Josh was standing up for Karinne.

The door opened, and Deputy Miller strode in, a pair of handcuffs in his grip. He glanced into the mirror as he grabbed Josh's arm and twisted it behind him, clamping the cuffs onto his wrists with the efficiency of a cop who'd done it a hundred times before. He grabbed Josh's wrist and tugged him toward the door. "Let's go, Mr. Magness. I have a nice suite for you in the back of the building. You'll be only slightly uncomfortable there for a while." As they headed through the door, I heard the young deputy say, "Room service sucks, but if you like burgers and fries, the food is decent."

Arno held up a finger, telling me to stay where I was, and then followed Miller through the door.

19

I paced the small room until Arno came in. He set his phone onto the wide sill of the viewing window and spoke. "Okay, Amity, what do you think?"

"Honestly," Hal said, his deep voice sounding slightly tinny through the phone. "I have no idea. There are a lot of things pointing at Josh Magness. There's no doubt about that. But his reaction to hearing where you found the gun makes me wonder."

"He could just be a good actor," Arno said.

"I don't think he was acting," I said.

Arno held my gaze for a beat. "Do you think you can be objective?"

Like Hal, I didn't know. "I'm trying to be." I glared at him. "Thanks, by the way, for the heads up on his identity."

Arno had the good sense to look guilty. "I'm sorry, Joey. But the last I heard, you weren't sure he was your brother. After seeing him face to face, I can definitely see the resemblance." He scrubbed a hand over his face. It was a mannerism I'd seen a hundred times, and it meant he was frustrated and maybe a little tired. "What do we think about

Karinne Magness? She was molested by Robb. It was her car that was spotted at the scenes. And she was in the vicinity when you found Calliente's body."

I could see the case Arno was trying to make. There was just one problem. "I'd agree with you that she was a possibility if Robb was our victim. But he isn't."

"We always seem to come back to that," Arno said.

And then there was my encounter in the dark the night before. "There's something I haven't told either of you yet," I said, eyeing the phone. Hal was going to be mad that I hadn't called him the night before. But he'd just have to get over it. I'd made the decision that was logical at the time. "I had a visitor last night when I had Caphy out for her final tour."

"Visitor?" Arno asked. "Who was it?"

With my guilty thoughts, the silence coming from the phone felt angry. I shoved guilt away. "I don't know who. He snuck up on me in the dark, down by the pond. I didn't see him, but I can guarantee it wasn't Karinne. It was definitely a man." A realization hit me hard and fast, and I nearly smiled. It couldn't have been Josh either. "It was a big man, strong and tall. It wasn't Joshua."

"You're sure?" Arno asked.

"As sure as I can be without seeing a face."

"What did he do?" Hal asked. The words emerged from him like nails from a nail gun. Oh yeah. He was mad.

"He didn't hurt me. He just held me so I couldn't turn around and see his face. And he threatened to hurt everybody I cared about if I didn't get my nose out of this investigation."

Arno stared at me as if perplexed. "Why?" he asked, clearly exasperated. "Why is it always you they go after?"

I'd pondered that myself and there was only one

possible explanation. I didn't like it. But I was pretty sure it was the truth. "They likely figure I'm the weak link. They think that if they can scare me enough, I'll get Hal to back down too."

Arno arched a brow. "Aren't you forgetting somebody?"

"They can't exactly stop the police from investigating, but at least they can limit the damage by getting rid of us."

"In this case," Hal interjected, "you have Mulhern working on shutting you down."

Arno had to agree. "He's getting to be a real pain in my a…"

"Welcome to our world," I said, cutting him off. "The sheriff has been a pain in our posteriors for months."

"Why's he so determined to protect this guy?" Hal asked.

"They've been friends for decades. Mulhern once said something about Robb saving his life. I don't think he meant it literally, but they've got a lot of history."

"Who do you *think* it was last night?" Hal asked me.

I didn't hesitate. "Mayor Robb."

"I think we have to go with the assumption that the person who *attacked* you is our killer," Hal said.

I didn't like the emphasis he put on 'attacked,' but I let it slide. I'd hear from him about it later. I'd deal with it then. "I was thinking the same thing. So we need to find out who could have been there around that time."

Arno inclined his head. "We already know Josh Magness could have been there, Joey."

I chewed my lip and kept my opinion to myself.

"I'll speak to Robb and check into the Magness parents," Arno said, surprising me.

"The parents?"

"Fathers sometimes do bad things to protect their daughters," Arno said.

He was right. I had trouble seeing Mr. Magness killing someone, but he *had* threatened to shoot my dog.

"I'll check into Benson Dexter, and Cecily Addams," Hal said.

"Cecily?" Surely he didn't think Cecily had attacked me at my home?

"We have to exclude everyone who is even remotely suspect," Arno told me.

I sighed. "Agreed."

"Any luck with ballistics on that gun?" Hal asked Arno.

"No, I sent it to Indianapolis for a complete forensics workup, but even before we get the ballistics report, I can tell you it's probably a community gun."

"What's that?" I asked.

"It's a gun that's hidden somewhere several people, usually gang members, can get hold of it when they need a weapon for unlawful purposes. When they're done with the weapon they put it back in its hiding spot until the next guy needs it. The firearm is usually illegally purchased and unidentifiable. We had one come through here last year. Unfortunately, we never caught the guy who used it to kill a pharmacy clerk in Bloomington. He passed through Deer Hollow, had a shootout on highway sixty-five with a rival gang member, and threw the gun out the window when he heard sirens heading his way. We'd have never found it except that the gun didn't quite make it into the grass."

"There's no serial number?" Hal asked.

"Filed off," Arno answered. "Still, the ballistics should give us a list of the places where the gun's been used. It might help us pinpoint our killer."

"I can run it up to Indy if you'd like," Hal offered. "I need to stop into the office and get some paperwork on a new case for Amity Investigations."

"Thanks. But Mulhern's taking it. He should just about be there by now."

"Okay. I'll set up my interviews. Has Prince woken up yet?"

Arno sighed. "Not yet. If he does, I'll let you know. Maybe you and Joey can talk to him since you've already approached him on an informal basis."

"Sounds good. Talk to you soon."

Hal disconnected without speaking to me again. Yep. He was ticked. Quick regret made my stomach twist, and then anger slid in to mute it. I wasn't a child, and I had a right to make decisions for myself. If he chose to be overprotective, that was on him. Not me.

I headed out of the building, nurturing that anger as long as I could because I knew as soon as it faded, the guilt would return. I pushed out into the midday sunshine with a sigh. I'd end up apologizing to my PI for not calling him. Even though his protective nature sometimes grated. More often, it was a comfort. And I knew it was meant to be a show of love.

My stomach growled as I pulled out of the station. I realized with a start that I hadn't had breakfast. Suddenly, I thought I was going to die if I didn't eat soon. I considered what I had at home to eat and made a quick decision. I'd drive into Deer Hollow and have lunch at the diner.

Or I'd pile another bad decision onto the one from last night and just have pie for lunch. Yeah. I liked the sound of that. As bad ideas went, it was a pretty good one.

Two people stood on the sidewalk, just down from Sonny's Diner. They had their heads together in what looked like a tense conversation.

Tiffany Brooks' platinum blonde hair made her easy to identify. She looked unhappy.

I drove slowly past, eyeing her companion, who I quickly realized was Martin Robb. Parking my Jeep well down the road, I climbed out and stood watching the pair.

Their expressions filled with anger, the couple seemed to be having quite the disagreement. Reaching out, Robb grabbed Tiffany's arm and gave her a little shake.

She yanked out of his grasp and said something I couldn't understand. But her body language and the unhappy look on her perfect features told me she hadn't liked whatever he'd said to her.

She took a step toward the diner, and he moved to cut her off. Using his larger form, He stepped into her, forcing her back and toward the alley between Sonny's and the new flower shop next door.

It was time for me to step in. I hurried to the sidewalk and called out. "Mayor Robb?"

Robb bent close and said something to Tiffany, his body language aggressive and angry.

She glared up at him and then gave him a shove.

"Mayor Robb!" I called again, louder the second time.

Tiffany looked past him at me. I motioned for her to go. She shot me a grateful look, turned on her heel, and hurried toward a snappy silver sports car I remembered from the last time we'd run into Tiffany at Sonny's.

"Mayor Robb?" I called out again.

He spun on me, his attractive face unrecognizable beneath the rage. "What do you want, Fulle? Why are you harassing me?"

I made a point of letting my less-than-genuine smile drift away. "I just wanted to tell you I'm sorry if we caused you any problems. Sheriff Mulhern told us we'd bothered you. That wasn't our intent, I promise."

Tiffany's little car swung away from the curb and accelerated up the street, heading out of town at a speed that was well above the thirty miles per hour limit.

I barely fought off a smug grin when Robb's jaw tightened at the sight. He was a bully with women, and I was glad to have cost him a victim. "She looks upset. Is everything all right?"

His mouth worked like he was chewing on a lot of bad words, and I was pretty sure I heard teeth grinding together. "What can I help you with, Ms. Fulle?"

I knew I was treading a very fine line. As soon as I left, Robb would no doubt get on the phone with his best buddy, Sheriff Mulhern and tattle on me for daring to speak to him on the street. I didn't care. With any luck, Robb would be in jail soon. "Not a thing. I really just wanted to apologize for intruding on you."

His dark brows lowered. "By intruding on me again?"

I let a smile curve my lips. "Yes. Well. I'm off to eat lunch."

I stopped with my hand on the door handle, turning back to him. "Mayor Robb?"

He stopped in mid-stride and dropped his head, a victim of my endless harassment. It was quite an act. "What?" he bit out.

"I was just wondering. When you were at the Fawn Hotel with Ms. Brooks the day Pam Wickham was killed, did you happen to notice anyone lurking around the hotel who shouldn't have been there?" It wasn't a throwaway question. I wanted to know if he'd seen my brother watching the place.

He turned around, fixing me with a cool, assessing gaze. "I thought you were told to stay off this case."

I inclined my head. "I was."

"And yet here you are, asking more questions about it."

"Sir, do you always do as you're told?"

He looked stunned for a moment, and then a new emotion crossed his face. Something that could have been real amusement. "No. I don't. Nobody who's worth knowing lets others tell them how to live their lives."

If the sentiment had come from anybody else, I'd have agreed wholeheartedly. But I was afraid Robb applied that logic to dealing with women who didn't want his attentions.

In a split-second decision that I hoped I didn't come to regret, I leveled with him. "Someone who's important to me is mixed up in these murders. I don't have it in me to sit back and let them get railroaded. If you can tell me anything that will help, I'd be very grateful."

If Robb was the murderer, he'd either claim ignorance or point the finger of blame at someone else. If he was innocent, maybe he'd tell me something I didn't know that might be helpful.

He stared at me for a long moment. I started to believe he wasn't going to answer my question. But he finally said, "Tiffany saw Pam Wickham fighting with someone when she came back from breakfast."

"Did she see who it was?" I asked.

"She couldn't describe the person. But she said it was a woman." He frowned. "She said she recognized the woman but couldn't quite place her." He looked concerned about that.

"Is that bad?"

He shook his head. "I just keep thinking that it's odd, that's all. Tiffany lives in Indianapolis. She doesn't know anyone here in Deer Hollow. That means either she was mistaken and she didn't know the woman, or someone followed her here from Indy." He rubbed a hand over his jaw, the slight stubble making a crackling sound. "That's odd, don't you think?"

"Small world?" I said, giving him a weak smile.

"Not that small," he disagreed. He turned and strode toward his fancy sports car without another word, leaving me with new questions and zero answers.

I suddenly wondered when Josh had blacked out the camera near Pam's room. Had it been clear earlier in the day? If so, I could maybe discover who Pam had been fighting with before her murder. "What time did Tiffany see this argument?" I called out.

He shrugged. "She's a late sleeper. If she went out for breakfast, it was probably ten-thirty or so when she left. I don't know when she came back."

Making a sudden decision, I pulled the door open and hurried into Sonny's. Ten minutes later, I was back in my car and doing a U-turn in the middle of Main Street.

With any luck, Victoria Lass would be in her office and she could show me video of the timeframe I was looking for.

20

"**M**s. Fulle. I'm surprised to see you again." The manager's smile was forced, and I couldn't help noticing how she glanced toward the door as if she expected someone else to come through it. "Is Mr. Amity joining you?"

I bristled at the implication that I needed him there. "Nope. Not today. I was wondering if I could view the security feed again?"

She blinked in surprise. "Oh. Um. Of course. But there wasn't much to see."

I smiled tightly. "If you'll queue it up for me, I'll be in and out as quickly as I can."

After a tense moment of hesitation, Victoria inclined her head. "Come with me."

I looked around the office while the manager found the feed we'd reviewed before. Ms. Lass hadn't put a lot of herself into the room. The narrow wall of built-in bookshelves was covered in non-fiction texts about improving management skills, customer service, and PR practices in the hotel industry, all reads that were likely as dry as desert air. I did see a few well-worn novels on the bottom shelf and itched to look at them to see what a serious, professional woman like Victoria Lass liked to read in her free time.

"There you go," she announced, rising from her chair. "I'll leave you to it. I have some details to see to at the front desk."

"Thank you," I told the other woman, standing back until she passed. I seated myself at her desk as she reached the door.

Victoria turned back to me as I began to scroll backward through the feed. "This has been very upsetting," she told me.

I looked up in surprise, thinking for just a beat that she was referring to my looking at the security feed. "I'm sorry?"

She flipped a well-manicured hand in the general direction of the rooms. "These murders. Our reservations have dropped by thirty percent almost overnight." She frowned, and my heart hurt for her. "We're trying to find the culprit," I assured her. "The sooner we do that, the sooner you can recover."

She nodded, her brow furrowing. "I don't suppose..."

I waited for her to finish, but she seemed to change direction. "Mr. Medford is very unhappy with me." Her form sagged as if the admission had wrung her dry.

I had a flash of intuition. She wanted me to speak to him for her. "None of this is your fault."

She shook her head. "I'd love to accept that, but I've been lax in the area of security. He's right to blame me."

"Garland Medford is the last person to blame someone else for things outside their control. Nothing in your experience would have led you to believe those murders would happen. He'll want you to adjust and change accordingly, but Garland wouldn't punish you for something you couldn't have seen coming. He's not that kind of person."

She relaxed slightly, nodding. "Thank you for that. I hope you're right."

"I am," I said, sounding more certain than I felt. I made a decision right then to speak to Garland on the woman's behalf after we caught the murderer. Assuming Victoria Lass wasn't in any way involved, of course.

She left me to my perusal of the feed, and I got right to it. Going back over the parking lot footage again, I noticed the same things we'd seen before, my chest tightening when I spotted Joshua parked under that tree. The camera scanned the lot and, though a couple of the cars seemed vaguely familiar, nothing new cropped up. I'd probably just seen the cars in town or at Martin Robb's party since it seemed a few of his guests had chosen to stay over at the Fawn.

Satisfied we hadn't missed anything there, I switched perspectives and scanned backward through the hours of the day, going just slowly enough that I'd see what I was looking for.

I found it around the ten AM mark.

Pammie Wickham appeared on the wooden walkway and started for her room. She was wearing running clothes and sneakers, her dark hair pulled back in a messy ponytail. Before Pammie reached her room, a woman stepped out of the shadows, cutting her off.

Pam jerked to a surprised stop, one hand flying to her mouth. Clearly, she hadn't known the woman was there. Unfortunately, her visitor was half-hidden by shadow. But something about her movements seemed familiar. I squinted at the recording but couldn't quite make out the second woman's features. She was obviously angry. Her movements were stiff and aggressive, and, for a moment, she put Pam Wickham back on her heels.

But then Pam seemed to pull herself up and she moved close, stabbing a finger toward the woman who'd surprised her. The two women appeared to indulge in a screaming match for a few minutes, and then Pam shoved past her assailant, nearly sending the other woman to the ground with the force of her shove.

With a final shouted word over her shoulder, Pammie Wickham opened the door of her room and stepped inside. The door slammed closed behind her.

I watched as the woman stepped out of the shadows, gasping when I saw her face clearly for the first time.

Cecily Addams.

Well now. That was a worm in the apple for sure.

HAL DIDN'T ANSWER his phone. I tried him several times on the way to Cecily's home. Panic clawed at my throat as I remembered that she'd been on Hal's interview list for the day. I told myself it would be okay. Surely, Cecily Addams wasn't a killer. Even if she was, she wouldn't stand a chance against Hal, right? He was smart and fast and...he had no idea Cecily might be dangerous.

I suddenly had trouble breathing, and my foot pressed harder on the gas. He wouldn't be expecting Cecily to be the killer. I'd heard it in his voice when he'd told Arno he'd talk to her. He was dotting all the I's, clearing suspects. She could easily catch him off guard.

Why wasn't he answering his dang phone?!

Buried in my thoughts and worries, I didn't notice the siren wailing behind me at first. By the time I looked in the mirror to find it, the sheriff's vehicle was riding way too close to my bumper. With the sun glancing off the windshield, I couldn't even tell who was driving.

Fear formed what felt like a fist-sized knot in my throat. Fear for Hal. Fear that I wouldn't be able to talk whoever was driving the cruiser into letting me go. Or even better, talk them into coming with me to make sure my PI was okay.

I pulled over and fought the urge to open the door. Police etiquette said such an action would be seen as a sign of aggression, and that was the last thing I wanted to do. In the mirror, I saw the big man saunter toward my car. I put my hands out of the window and started talking before he came even with the Jeep. "I'm sorry. I didn't hear the siren. You need to help me. I think Hal might be in trouble."

The big cop stopped near my open window, looking down at me with a glint in his brown eyes. "Joey Fulle. Where are you going in such a hurry?"

I squinted against the sun to look up at him. "I think Hal's talking to the killer. I can't reach him on the phone, and I'm really worried."

Sheriff Mulhern's eyes widened in surprise. "You found the killer?"

"I'm not sure. But I saw Pammie Wickham fighting with someone at the hotel right before she was killed. I'm pretty sure that person is the killer. We need to go." Panic flared as he took a moment to think about what I'd said. He was too slow. Too deliberative in his thinking.

"Please," I urged, not even sure I knew what I was begging him to do.

The sheriff tipped his hat back on his head. "Who's this person you think is the killer?"

In desperation, I did the only thing I could think of to get him moving. "I promise I'll tell you that, but we need to get moving."

He eyed me a moment longer and then reached for my door. "Ride with me. We can go faster with the sirens."

Relief swelled through me. I quickly climbed out of the car and started toward the sheriff's cruiser. "No SUV today?" I asked as he reached toward the door.

He laughed. "It's in the shop. Tell ya the truth, I really wish I had it." He pulled the door open for me.

"Really? I said, trying to smile. Is it more comfortable?"

His hand slipped toward his hip and came up holding a gun. Something mean and shifty passed through his eyes even as my brain struggled to make the switch. "No. It's better for hauling bodies." I saw the movement and barely had time to duck instinctively before the gun connected with my skull, and the world fell away.

Jeezopete! My head's killing me. I was lying on something smooth and lumpy that smelled like manure. The space where I'd been dumped was like a sauna. It was so hot, my clothing was drenched and my hair stuck to my face and neck in dripping clumps.

I'd been working my way toward consciousness for a while, but there was a narrow beam of light coming from somewhere, and every time I tried to open my eyes, that light drilled a hole in them, forcing me to slam them closed again.

My whole body was sore as if I'd been dragged behind a

horse for a few miles. I tried to shift into a more comfortable position, but my wrists and ankles were bound together with something and my balance was off. I kept nose-diving back to my lumpy perch.

In the distance, muffled voices had been keeping up a running commentary for a good part of my pain-filled awareness.

"...can't believe you brought her here!"

"What did you want me to do with her? This is your mess I'm trying to clean up."

I focused on the words that I could suddenly hear more clearly. My battered brain slowly settled on the knowledge that the two men I could hear were moving closer.

As soon as I realized that, I started to struggle.

"What do you plan to do with her?" the man with Mulhern asked on a harsh whisper.

"I'm gonna take her to the river."

If I was panicked before, the sheriff's cold, merciless tone propelled me to new levels of anxiety. *Not the river!* Falling beneath the roiling surface of the Fawn River and being dragged to the murky bottom in the water's icy embrace was my worst nightmare. I'd rather take a bullet to the head than drown in the river.

I pushed against the foul-smelling surface beneath me and almost managed to sit up. Dizziness swamped me, turning the world into a carnival ride that threatened to bring up the contents of my stomach.

I slammed back down just as a metallic shriek warned me that Mulhern and friend had arrived in my prison. There was nothing to do but play like I was still unconscious. I'd look for an opportunity to escape somewhere along the way to the Fawn.

Think, Joey! I admonished myself. I assessed every

small detail available and decided I was somewhere on the mayor's large property. I tried to remember if the river crossed nearby. I thought it did, a realization that squeezed my lungs with icy fingers, making it hard to breathe.

I needed time.

Time and luck.

Hal and Arno would surely realize I was missing. Somebody would find my car abandoned alongside the road. Could they track my cell phone, which was *dangit!* still sitting in the console of my car? Why hadn't I thought to grab my phone? But, even if they found my car, how would they know where to look for me?

Despair threatened to send me into a full-blown panic attack. I struggled to breathe while still trying to fake unconsciousness.

"How are we going to explain that she's missing? That boyfriend of hers will know something funny happened."

"Don't worry about Amity. He's next on my list."

Ruthless hands snagged me off the ground and threw me over an unrelenting shoulder. I grunted and fought the sensation that I couldn't fill my lungs with enough air. "He'll be only too eager to come with me when I tell him I think I know where his pretty little girlfriend is."

I barely kept from groaning. Mulhern was right. Hal would come with him in a heartbeat. He'd have no reason to doubt the sheriff's intentions.

I gave up trying to act unconscious and started to wriggle and kick. Unfortunately, trussed up like a Christmas turkey, I couldn't do much except make the sheriff laugh.

"Are you sure this is necessary?"

I was getting pretty sick of Robb's whiny voice. "You aren't going to get away with this," I warned as I tried to kick

Mulhern in the crotch. I was off target by about six inches, barely grazing his thigh.

Mulhern opened the back door of the cruiser and threw me inside. I hit the slick plastic of the back seat hard enough to knock the air out of my lungs. I wheezed miserably, crumbling to the floor as I fought to breathe. "I already have, young lady. You might as well make peace with the fact that you and your PI are both dead."

"Good luck with that," Robb, the coward, said. "I want no part of this."

The sound of flesh smashing against flesh was distinct. Robb's body slammed into the side of the car and slid to the ground with the screech of leather against metal. Someone grunted, and I dragged myself back onto the seat in time to see Mulhern dragging Robb back up and slamming him against the car. He got in the other man's face, his thick finger stabbing against Robb's chest. "You created this mess. You. Not me. By killing Calliente. I'm helping you clean it up. And let there be no misunderstandings on this. I expect your money and your influence in my corner during my campaign this fall. You owe me, big time."

Robb held up his hands. "You got it. I understand."

I nearly swallowed my tongue. Mulhern was going to kill Hal and me so he could get re-elected as sheriff? Seriously?

The sheriff shoved Robb away from the car and slid behind the wheel, glancing at me. "Ready to go for a swim?"

He took off so fast, it threw me back against the hard seat. Sending dirt and gravel into the air, Mulhern took the turn onto the road as if he were being chased by the hounds of Hell.

I was flung backward as he hit the gas and accelerated down a gravel road I didn't recognize. I turned to look back at Mayor Robb, finding him standing next to a metal shed that was no doubt used to store fertilizer and other gardening implements. The man stood with his shoulders rounded, his gaze locked on us as we tore away from him.

I wondered if he was regretting getting mixed up with Mulhern. No matter what happened to Hal and me, he was going to be looking over his shoulder for a long, long time.

21

As I suspected, the river wasn't far enough away. Mulhern raced down one dirt road after another and then slammed the car to a stop near a group of old-growth trees at the edge of the churning Fawn.

I stared in horror at the foamy water, knowing that the worst of the agitation was beneath the surface, unseen and oh-so-deadly.

The spot he'd brought me to was a small inlet with a sandy shoreline, which would have been pretty if I hadn't come there to die.

In the middle of the river, lashed incessantly by the churning water, was a tangle of uprooted trees and broken branches that had been driven together by the current and seemed to be stuck there. I wondered if I could make it to that prickly island of relative safety before I drowned.

Swimming would be nearly impossible with my ankles and wrists bound. I had to try to talk him into taking them off.

The door groaned open and I tried to scrabble away

from his grip, finding my escape halted way too fast by the other door.

Mulhern reached inside and grabbed a flailing ankle, brutally yanking me out of the car. I slammed to the ground hard enough to draw a pained wheezing sound from my lungs, my tailbone screaming from the impact.

The sheriff yanked me up and threw me over his shoulder again, barely noticing my fists slamming against his back and my feet smashing into the unyielding wall of his middle. The man might be a douche canoe of the highest order, but he had some rock-hard abs.

"What are you going to do with me?" I asked, playing dumb. Maybe I could get him talking and postpone the inevitable for a bit.

He threw me onto the sandy beach, where I discovered the sand was merely an illusion. It was about half an inch thick over what felt like rocks and hard dirt.

Agony speared through my back at the impact. My tailbone gave a sharp yowl of irritation and my head, which had never stopped screaming, took a moment to pound sharp nails into my brain.

I lay there a long moment, agony making it hard to breathe or think.

To my shock, Mulhern bent over me and cut the ties off my limbs. "I thought we'd already covered that."

Breathing through the pain, I forced myself to sit up. If I was going to have a chance to survive, I was going to need to make a run for it.

The thought made all my bruised parts sing a chorus of resistance.

"Can we talk about what's happening?" I asked him. "I don't even know why you're doing this. I don't know anything that can hurt you or Robb. I haven't learned anything at all." *Except that they were both jerks of the highest order and probably killers.*

Mulhern walked around the trees, his gaze skimming the ground.

Seeing my chance, I tried to stand.

He reached out and shoved me back down, faster than I'd expected. Apparently, he was still paying attention despite his search for whatever he was looking for under the trees.

I fell into a puddle of agony on the rock-like beach.

"Feel free to talk all you want. But you're still gonna die," he told me.

"But, why?"

He bent and picked up a piece of branch. It was about 24 inches long and three inches in diameter. He smacked it against his palm, testing it. Unfortunately, it looked solid.

"Because I can control my cops. I can point them in the wrong direction for these murders and make it stick. But I can't control you or your nosy boyfriend. So you both need to go."

"You don't think they'll look into our deaths?"

He shrugged. "You fell into the river and drowned. It's a tragedy. So close to your house." He jerked his head upriver. "You live just a couple of miles from here. It's a perfectly reasonable explanation."

A chill that had nothing to do with the temperature made my teeth clank together. "And Hal?"

"He tried to save you. Big strong guy like that, it's a shame he couldn't manage it. Unfortunately, the Fawn's a nasty witch. She's taken down even the strongest swimmers over the years."

With a sinking feeling that flared into nausea as I tried

again to stand, I knew he was right. Unless I found a way to push past the pain, I was going to die.

Mulhern strode toward me, the piece of branch clutched in his beefy hand. "I know you think I'm enjoying this, Joey. But, I assure you, I'm not."

I glared at him, not buying it for one second. In the blink of an eye, he'd reverted to his campaign persona. The kind, protective warrior with a gentle touch.

I nearly snorted at the mask he'd donned. And then it hit me. If he got away with killing me and my PI, that mask would be the reality for a couple of thousand people in Deer Hollow.

I couldn't let that happen.

"This will only hurt for a second," he assured me as his arm came up and a lethal smile creased his face.

Adrenaline swamped me, and I rolled away from the strike. I landed on a palm-sized rock and closed my fingers around it. Keeping it hidden with my body, I tugged on the rock, pulling it free of the sand. Mulhern stood over me again, his foot on my belly to hold me in place.

He lifted the branch, preparing to strike again, and rage joined the adrenaline in a potent cocktail that had me moving before my brain caught up to what I was going to do.

My hand with the rock came up, and I smashed it hard into his crotch.

Mulhern's hand stalled in midair, his eyes going wide and his face turning an ugly shade of puce. He stumbled backward, releasing me from his weight.

I rolled away from him as the branch fell from his grip and he doubled over, a strange keening sound escaping his lips.

I shoved to my knees and then to my feet. My brain

wobbled painfully inside my skull, but I ignored it, knowing I wouldn't get another chance. I ran into the trees, praying I could find my way home without getting lost.

Then it didn't matter if I was heading the right way because footsteps pounded after me, and I realized I'd wrung the only advantage I had out of the situation.

"Stop running, you stupid woman!" Mulhern bellowed.

The sound was like needles pricking my skin, and I knew if he caught me I was dead. As if to prove the point, a bullet smacked into the tree just ahead of me, bark and slivers of wood spitting from the resulting wound and slicing into my exposed flesh as I ran past. More bullets slammed around me. I couldn't run any faster, but I could run smarter, so I veered off the path and deeper into the trees in the hopes of avoiding a bullet to the back of the head.

Ahead of me, a strange howling sound made my steps falter, and I caught a root with my toe. The impetus of my run sent me flying. I hit the ground hard enough to knock the wind out of my lungs again. I lay there wheezing, frustrated tears sliding from my eyes.

Footsteps crashed through the trees behind me. Close. Too close.

I thought about trying to keep running but knew it was too late. Instead, I dragged myself into the brush, under a half-rotted tree that had fallen onto the rich loamy soil, and prayed Mulhern would pass me by before the millions of tiny insects feasting on the soft wood turned their sights on my poor exposed flesh.

I shuddered at the thought. A crawly sensation tickled along my calf, and I closed my eyes, pinching my lips closed to keep from screaming.

The thunderous footsteps slammed to a stop mere feet

away from where I hid. I barely breathed, knowing the slightest sound would bring him down on me.

"Where are you, Joey? You know you can't get away from me. I promise I'll make it quick."

He was a madman if he thought that was a compelling argument.

Something bit the soft skin at the back of my knee and, before I could stop myself, I made a soft sound of pain and slapped at the bug.

Mulhern's head shot up, and he turned to look at me. A horrible smile spread over his face. "Gotcha." He raised his gun, hand steady and eyes mean. "Buh bye."

The underbrush split and threw a muscular golden shape into the air. A feral snarl rolled over me, lifting every hair on my body to attention.

Caphy slammed into Mulhern as he pressed the trigger, and the bullet sailed above my head, smacking into a large, dead tree at my back.

Amid a barrage of vicious, wet snarls and the terrifying snapping of large, white teeth, Mulhern screamed like a girl and dropped the gun.

Another large form emerged from the trees. The man was tall, wearing a fearsome expression, and he was a wonderful sight to see.

"I'd advise you to go very still, Sheriff," Hal said, his tone colder than I'd ever heard it.

I turned my head to find Mulhern, bug-eyed and pale as a sheet, with pibl jaws wrapped around his throat. "Call her off, Amity," Mulhern whispered harshly.

"Joey?"

I rolled from my hiding spot and grabbed the gun Mulhern had dropped. "I'm okay." Mostly.

"Leave it, sweet girl," I told my dog.

Caphy hesitated another beat as if to let Mulhern know she could finish the job if necessary and then released him, trotting over to lick an ant off my knee.

I was dimly aware of Hal binding Mulhern's wrists behind his back as I dropped to my knees and buried my face in my dog's soft fur. "You saved me again," I said, my words thick with tears. "You're getting donuts every day for a month."

Caphy's tail whipped the air, and she panted happily.

"I've got him," Hal said.

I glanced up to find my PI yanking the sheriff off the ground with one hand and talking into his cell. "We'll meet you at the clearing."

Hal's gaze slid over me as I joined him, making sure to stay clear of Mulhern. "Are you sure you're all right?"

"I'm a little bruised and sore, but I'll be fine." I slapped at another ant, glaring at Mulhern. "Robb's in on all of it with him."

Hal gave a brisk nod. "We'll talk about it after we get him locked up."

"You don't have anything to charge me with," Mulhern said. He was either a really good actor, or he actually believed he'd get away with his crimes.

"I heard you and Robb talking about killing those people," I told him. "You kidnapped and tried to kill me."

Mulhern raised a dark brow. "That's strange. I have a different story to tell. I heard you screaming and came to try to rescue you. Unfortunately, your dog tried to kill me. I'll see that beast put down, Fulle. You have my word on that."

Could he do that? Surely he wouldn't walk away from two murders and two attempted murders? I dug my fingers into Caphy's fur and just concentrated on breathing.

"Nobody's touching that dog," Hal said, giving me a reassuring glance before turning a stone-cold stare toward Mulhern. "And you're going down for murder. Any way you paint it."

Mulhern was silent as we stepped into the clearing where Arno and his deputies waited.

When I glanced at Hal, he smiled. And then, unbelievably, he winked.

22

"You need to go to the hospital," Hal said for the fifth time. "You might have a concussion."

"I'm fine. The headache's not even that bad anymore." It wasn't a complete lie. The pain had changed from skull-shattering agony to only murderously miserable. A slight improvement. "Tell me how you found me in the middle of the woods."

"You can thank Caphy for that part. As soon as we hit the clearing, she took off running as if she knew exactly where you were. It was all I could do to keep up with her."

"How'd you know to look in the woods?"

"We didn't," Arno said, coming into his office and closing the door behind him. Caphy jumped up from her spot on the rug near my chair and ran over to greet him. "We tracked the cruiser to the river and planned to come in hot, with Hal keeping an eye on the back door in case Mulhern broke that way."

"We knew Caphy could catch him even if I couldn't," Hal said.

Arno cupped my dog's squishy face between his hands

and gave her an enthusiastic scratch under the chin and behind the ears. "Who's our good girl?"

I laughed as Caphy's entire body wagged in a delighted response.

Arno sat down behind his desk with a soft groan. "What a day."

"Tell me you have enough evidence to put Mulhern and Robb in jail."

Both Hal and Arno grinned widely.

"What?" I couldn't help it, I smiled too. Even though I had no idea what I was smiling about.

"We have the evidence to put them both in prison," Arno said. He waited a bit and then said, "Thanks to your brother."

My eyes went wide. "What does Josh have to do with this?"

"He was at Robb's place when Mulhern dragged you out of that shed. He'd been watching Robb's house and saw him come flying out, jump into his car, and tear down the road toward the back of the property," Hal said.

"Wait," I said. "I thought Josh was in jail."

Arno shook his head. "I released him after a couple of hours. I didn't have anything solid to keep him on, and I reminded him I'd be looking at his sister for the murders if he disappeared on me."

I stared at him in disbelief. "You threatened his sister?"

"She *was* a person of interest. And she appears to be on the run. If we hadn't caught the real killers, I'd have an APB out on her already," Arno said.

I shook my head. He was right. Even though I didn't like it.

"Anyway, Josh knew something was going on, so he followed Robb and caught the two men arguing about the mayor killing Calliente." If it was possible, Arno's smile widened. "Magness recorded it all. Every damning word of it."

Hal nodded. "We were already trying to find Mulhern. His SUV was in his garage at home, but he wasn't there."

"I'd gotten a call from the lab asking why the gun never arrived for its ballistics tests," Arno told me. "That was when I started to wonder what Mulhern was up to. I had a thought about that gun and checked it out. The community gun from the gang case was missing from the evidence room. We put two and two together and came up with Mulhern."

"Josh saw the sheriff pull me out of that shed?" I couldn't believe he'd been there. He could have gotten shot.

"He did," Arno responded. "He called me immediately. But, by the time he got into his car and took off after Mulhern, the cruiser was gone. Magness covered nearly every road out here but couldn't find you."

I nodded. Once he lost me, it would have been a miracle for him to find me again. The dirt roads out there were like a spider web. "So you tracked the cruiser and found us."

Arno nodded. "That brother of yours has a future as an investigator," he said.

"Or a cop," Hal suggested. "He was quick enough to get the number off the cruiser, so Arno didn't have to waste time figuring out which of the fleet Mulhern had borrowed for his little murder spree. After that, it was just a matter of tracking the car through GPS monitoring."

Hal touched my cheek with a warm finger. "Now tell us what happened out there."

I did, netting it out as quickly as I could and skipping over the parts where I thought I was going to die. I'd talk about those parts with Hal later. In private, where we could hold onto each other and celebrate the fact that we were both safe and alive.

"I'll be sure to thank Josh for coming to my rescue."

Hal nodded. "He knows who you are. He's apparently been watching you for a while. I guess he's been working up the courage to speak to you."

My mind played back pictures from a stormy night a few months earlier when I'd seen a man standing in my yard. A flash of lightning had illuminated the familiar features he'd taken from my dad. It had jolted me badly. At the time, I'd thought it was my father, returning from the grave. I hadn't been that far off after all.

I smiled as another piece of the puzzle fell into place. "That explains a few things," I said, sharing a knowing glance with Hal. "Okay," I said, changing the subject. "We know that Robb killed Calliente. But do we know why?"

Arno sighed. "Calliente threatened Robb for a big payoff when he found evidence in Robb's home. Robb clearly didn't handle the blackmail attempt well. He killed Calliente, believing the evidence was still in the house somewhere since Calliente hadn't left since arriving to set up for the party. Robb thought he had it contained and would find it later. But he didn't realize that Pammie Wickham had been at the house earlier. She wasn't there long. We're speculating that Calliente gave the evidence to her."

I grimaced. "What exactly did Calliente find?"

"A wooden cigar box filled with souvenirs of Robb's exploits, including the locket Karinne Magness reported stolen by Robb when he was running for City Councilman. Unbelievably, Robb kept women's barrettes, jewelry, lipstick, even underwear. We found the box in Anthony Prince's car, under about a year's worth of dirty laundry. Pam Wickham must have given it to him to hide for her after Calliente was killed."

I grimaced.

"I sent a deputy to the house after we pulled Robb in, and he said there was a dust-free rectangle on Robb's shelves that perfectly matches that box. The arrogant jerk left the box right out in plain sight."

"Ugh!" I said, dropping my face into my hands. "What a pig."

Arno nodded. "When Robb got back to the party, he pulled the sheriff aside and gave him a wild confession. I saw them talking and thought Robb looked upset but didn't put the pieces together until much later. Then I talked myself out of it as being too farfetched."

"Mulhern was counting on that reaction," I murmured. "He didn't think anybody would believe he was capable of murder."

"He was wrong," Hal said. "When we're done with him, people will not only believe he's a killer but that he also had something to do with the high cost of gasoline and skyrocketing inflation."

Laughing, I asked, "What about Cecily Addams?"

"What about her?" Hal asked.

"I went back to the Fawn Hotel and rewatched the tape."

"Why?" Arno asked.

Flushing with guilt, I admitted. "I ran into Mayor Robb in front of the diner earlier."

Arno shook his head. "You're impossible," he said, but his lips twitched.

"Whatever. Robb was harassing Tiffany Brooks. I distracted him so she could get away. He told me that Cecily and Pam got into a big fight right before Pam was killed, so I thought Cecily might have killed her." I looked at Hal. "I knew you were going to interview her. When you didn't answer your phone…"

He pulled me into a quick hug. "Sorry, honey. Things were breaking fast here. In all fairness, I had no idea you'd get yourself into trouble just driving home."

Arno snorted out a laugh.

"Har," I said.

"Anyway," Arno said, "Mulhern apparently agreed to cover for Robb with the investigation if Robb agreed to help get him re-elected as sheriff."

"See, Mulhern told me that too. But I don't get it. Why would he even worry about being reelected? He's popular enough, isn't he?"

Arno made a face. "On the surface. But recently, I've heard rumblings about the fact that he's so distant from everything that goes through the office. He's more interested in schmoozing with his influential buddies in Indy."

"Power always wants to grow," I said, nodding.

"It probably has as much to do with money as anything," Arno admitted. "Plus, Mulhern always intended to turn a sheriff's position into higher office. Politicians gotta politician."

"What our humble friend isn't telling you, Joey," Hal said, "Is that there's significant interest in him running against Mulhern for sheriff."

I squealed in delight. "Do it! You basically already do the job. People love and respect you around here. You're a shoo-in."

Arno wrenched his brows up in disbelief. "Love me?"

I chuckled. "Yes! Well, those of us who can see beyond the gruff, grumpy, crotchety…"

"All right," he said, laughing. "I get the picture. Besides, there isn't currently a sheriff to run against."

"Even better," Hal said, clapping him on the back.

"I wouldn't have the first idea how to run for office."

"Benson has offered to help you, right?" Hal said.

I clapped my hands, my delight doubling. "Benson can run for mayor again. He'd win too. Especially with Cecily helping him."

Arno put up his hands. "Let's not get ahead of ourselves."

"Okay," I agreed. "I'll table it for now. But I plan to harass you non-stop until you agree to run."

Arno grimaced.

"Now, tell me about Prince. How is he, by the way?"

"He's still out, but the doctors are hopeful. He's stable and showing signs of waking up."

"That's good," Hal said. "Hopefully, he'll be able to point the finger at whoever shot him when he comes to."

"It's a pretty good bet that Mulhern shot him," Arno said. "Prince had been spouting off that he knew a secret about Robb. We don't know how Mulhern found out about it, but we're speculating the sheriff decided Prince was a risk and went to kill him. Unfortunately for the sheriff, you two showed up before he could get out of Prince's room and he was forced to flee out the window."

Hal nodded. "What happened to Pam Wickham is a little more complex. She and Calliente were, as far as we can tell, blackmailing Mayor Robb over his disgusting and illegal activities. I don't know how long it had been going on, but I suspect, since Calliente Catering had done several events that Robb either hosted or attended, she and her fiancé had been watching Robb spin his filthy web with numerous women for a while."

"When the box of damning evidence didn't turn up at

Robb's place," Arno said, "Wickham was the obvious person to confront over where it was."

"Benson said he offered to pay Calliente for information on Robb," I reminded them.

"Which was likely icing on the cake for the blackmailing duo," Hal said. "They'd already extorted Robb into paying them in cash and connections. Getting paid by Benson Dexter was a fortuitous new development."

"Ooh," I said, teasing. "Fortuitous. A ten-dollar word. Very sexy."

Hal gave me a small bow. "I aim to titillate."

"Okay," Arno said, holding up a hand. "There will be no titillating in my office."

I giggled.

"However the extortion went down," Hal said, "it's clear that Robb saw the opportunity to rid himself of the other half of his Calliente problem."

"Why didn't Robb just kill Wickham instead of involving the sheriff? I asked. "He clearly knew where she was." I thought about the security video I'd seen where he looked up to the room above Tiffany's.

Arno shook his head. "As you know, he was at the hotel when she was killed. My guess is he saw the opportunity to kill her before she went back to Indy. But he couldn't afford to be blamed for the murder. He used Tiffany Brooks as his alibi and called Mulhern to do his dirty work again."

"I bet the sheriff was getting pretty sick of the guy at that point," I said.

"No doubt," Arno agreed. "This is where it gets interesting. We know that Joshua Magness painted over the camera on that part of the balcony."

I nodded. "He'd intended to search Pam's room the next time she was out and didn't want to be caught on video."

"Exactly," Arno agreed. "Apparently, Mulhern took note of the blacked-out camera and knew he couldn't be seen. He talked his way into Wickham's room..."

"Not exactly a difficult task with her," Hal murmured.

"Right," Arno agreed. "He turned up the music to cover the sounds of the struggle and made quick work of her. Then he turned off the music and, as we saw from the parking lot feed, was back in his car less than twenty minutes later."

"What about the fictitious maid?" I asked. "We couldn't find a maid who'd talked to him."

"That's because he never talked to one. The maid was just his excuse for not finding the freshly murdered body of Pam Wickham," Arno said.

"Wow, I said. These people are quite the nest of vipers, aren't they?"

"It's hard to imagine that anybody will miss any of them," Arno agreed.

"Okay," Hal said, catching me rubbing my temples with my fingers. "Let's get you to the hospital."

"I don't want to," I whined.

But he wasn't having any of it. "I'll drop you off at the Emergency room and run the Beauty home. It's too hot for her to stay in the car."

"Leave her here," Arno said.

"Are you sure?" I asked.

"Of course. She's good company. And if Sheppard comes in and tries to read one of his two-hundred-page reports to me, I can sic her on him."

"You will not!" I exclaimed as Hal urged me toward the door.

"Joey," the cop said, feigning hurt. "What kind of cad do you take me for? I was just kidding."

I shook my head as Hal opened the door.

"I'll just dump gravy over his head and let her lick him into submission."

"Uh..." I started to object.

Hal pushed me gently through the door and closed it behind us.

WE STEPPED out into the late afternoon sunshine and I stopped, closing my eyes and pulling air into my lungs. My focus on the pounding pain of my headache retreated for a beat, taking a temporary backseat to the joy of being alive.

Hal touched my shoulder. "Should I go get the car?"

I started to shake my head and then remembered why I was headed to the hospital as the action sent piercing pain through my skull and radiating down my spine. "No. Just give me a minute."

He kissed my temple. "Wait here."

I let him go because it suddenly felt like too much trouble to move. I stood there, letting the heat of the sun soothe the aches stabbing me in several places.

"Joey?"

My eyes shot open. I looked into the gray-blue gaze of my brother, standing five feet away and looking sheepish. "Josh."

His lips curved in a tentative smile. "You know who I am."

"I do. Thank you. For helping them find me in time."

He wrung his hands together, looking at his feet as though embarrassed. "It seemed like the least I could do." He stuck his hands in the pockets of his jeans and frowned. "I wanted to apologize for that phone call."

"Phone call?"

"About Robb. I realized after I hung up that it had probably sounded like a threat. I was only trying to warn you that you were in danger."

Understanding bloomed in my battered mind. He was referring to the strange call that told me Robb had dangerous friends. "Ah. *That* phone call." I grimaced. "It was a little disconcerting. But thanks for the warning. I think."

He shook his head. "I also apologize for stalking your house. I promise I was only curious."

Stalking? His words made *me* curious. "I don't understand."

"When the cops picked me up, I was just returning to the car from your house."

My eyes went wide. "You were at my house? Why didn't I see you?"

He shrugged. "Probably because I was hiding in the trees. I like your house. Your pets. Your life. I like to imagine what it had been like for you, growing up in that house. In this town. When you and Mr. Amity came home, I left. I didn't want your dog to find me."

"But why stand out in the yard? Why not come talk to me?"

"I didn't know how you'd react to the news of having a long lost brother. From the moment I learned I had another family, my parents have been telling me that you didn't want to know about me. I thought I was being selfish, wanting to get to know you." He looked down at his shoes, his color rising. "I didn't want to mess up your life."

His thoughts so closely mirrored mine, it made my heart twist with hurt.

Kicking the metal leg of a nearby bench with his sneaker, Josh avoided my gaze. When he looked up again, his face held a hopeful expression. "I was wondering if we could grab lunch sometime...maybe talk."

Tears flooded my eyes and I smiled. "I'd like that."

He grinned. "Really?"

I nodded. "I'd like it a lot."

"Good. I'll call you?" he offered.

"Yes." I didn't ask him if he had my number. I knew he did. Arno was right. Joshua Magness should be a cop or an investigator. I added that to the list of things we would talk about and the thought made everything in my world feel right again. "I'll see you soon, then?"

"You will." He turned to go as Hal drove up to the curb. "Bye, Joey."

I pulled air into my lungs and sighed it out as Josh walked away. My smile trembled a bit and was accompanied by tears, but they were happy tears. "See you soon, Josh," I whispered.

And then I climbed into the car, scrubbing at the tears sliding down my cheeks.

I had a brother. And I couldn't wait to get to know him.

The End

DON'T MISS OUT

Stay up on all Sam's news by joining her newsletter, and get a copy of a fun mystery just for signing up!

SIGN UP HERE!
https://samcheever.com/newsletter/

READ MORE COUNTRY COUSIN MYSTERIES

If you enjoyed **Distinguished Bumpkin** you might want to check out the next book in the series: https://samcheever. com/books/#Country

Enjoy this taste of Book 10: **Rumble Bumpkin.**

Not since the days when Vlad the Impaler rampaged the quaint countryside of Wallachia Romania, has anyone deserved to go to prison more than George Shulz. Unfortunately, we have to prove he did something wrong first.

Self-proclaimed sociopathic lawyer George Shulz is a cross between the "get off my lawn" guy and Hannibal Lecter. A less likable individual would be hard to find in Deer Hollow. So, when he's arrested at the site of a recent murder involving a missing deer, Shulz's car, and a body with a clear set of tire tracks painting his backside, there doesn't seem to be much question whether he's guilty.

Everybody wants him to be.

Unfortunately, for everybody, Shulz keeps insisting he didn't do it. And worse, he wants me, Joey Fulle, and my boyfriend Hal, the PI, to prove his innocence.

I really just have a hankerin' to grab a pitchfork and join the lynch mob.

Unfortunately for me, Hal and his brother Cal are on the job, intending to prove the horrible man's innocence.

Dangit!

On the plus side, I get to spend some quality time with my bestie, Felicity, from the big city.

But I'm thinkin' I might occasionally drift over to the torch and pitchfork side, just for fun.

RUMBLE BUMPKIN

No really," I told the cranky Siamese cat who was currently draped across my underwear. "You can't come with. I promise we'll only be gone a day. Just twenty-four little hours. It will be fine. Lis is going to come stay with you, Caphy, and Ethel Squeaks." I reached out and gently poked the cat's sleek hip, earning a heartfelt hiss for my efforts.

I sighed. "You like Lis. I know you do."

"Woowoowoo," sang my blonde, green-eyed Pitbull. Caphy topped off her song by licking my ankle.

"See," I told the perennially unhappy feline, "Caphy likes Lis."

LaLee snapped her tail against my hand and then got gracefully to her feet, turned her back on me, and flopped back down on top of my favorite satin and lace bra.

I sighed. My cell rang and I glanced over to see my boyfriend Hal's picture on the screen. The photo was inspiring. I was glad for the hundredth time that I'd taken the time to figure out how to personalize his calls with his own picture. "Hey," I said with a smile. "Are you on your way?"

"I'm getting gas. I'll pick up Ethel Squeaks and be there

in fifteen minutes. Are you ready?" I ignored the doubt threading his deep voice. If he doubted my ability to prepare to leave town on a tight timetable, he wasn't wrong. But I couldn't rush my fashion choices. I was competing with my cousin, Felicity's perfect fashion sense. I needed to give myself plenty of options.

Grimacing, I said, "I'm *almost* ready. I might need to bring the cranky feline with me, though. She's refusing to leave my suitcase."

He chuckled. "That sounds about right. I've got another call. I'll see you in a few minutes. Be the alpha."

Be the alpha. I sighed. I had no problem being the alpha. But I'd probably only have power over a pack of one. Caphy would happily let me pretend I was in charge. But LaLee would scoff at the idea that anyone could be alpha over her.

Ceding defeat on the suitcase, I decided to go pack my makeup bag instead. Maybe LaLee would get bored if I wasn't there for her to annoy and she'd leave.

Hope sprang eternal.

I went into the bathroom and brushed out my shoulder-length, red-blonde hair, pulling it up into a high ponytail before examining my lightly-tanned oval face in the mirror and deciding a little blush and eyeliner to set off the blue of my eyes wouldn't be a bad idea.

My phone rang before I had all my toiletries laid out to pack. It was Hal again.

"Please tell me you're not here already." I hurriedly started shoving stuff into my bag.

"Unfortunately, no. And it doesn't look as if we're going to Indianapolis today."

I stopped shoving, disappointed. "What's up?"

A door slammed on the other end of the line, and I figured that Hal had gotten out of his car. The sound of wind soughing through the connection verified it. "Arno called me in on a potential case," he responded.

I sagged down onto the closed toilet seat, my disappointment tripling. "So, probably no Indianapolis for a while then?"

He must have heard the disappointment in my voice. "I'm sorry, honey. But I could use your help with something. Or, really Caphy's help. Would you mind coming out here and bringing her with you?"

I perked up. "To the crime scene?" I glanced toward my bedroom, where my pibl was currently pawing at the mattress near my suitcase to make LaLee wobble. The feline hissed enthusiastically with every vibration, a circumstance that only spurred Caphy to greater heights of pawing. Her tail wagged manically at the cat's very satisfying reaction, her pretty green eyes bright with pleasure. "You sure you want to unleash the pibl on a crime scene?"

Hal greeted someone on the other end of the line, but I couldn't decipher the answering rumble of a response. Then my PI returned to our conversation. "I have to go, honey." He quickly gave me his location and reminded me to bring my dog.

I disconnected with a sigh, watching Caphy twist herself into half a pretzel before slamming her paw down on the mattress and launching LaLee out of the suitcase. The cat landed on her tiny, dark paws and shot off the bed, hissing heartily as Caphy did celebratory zoomies around the room.

Despite my frustration at missing our outing to Indy, I grinned at my dog's antics. Then I climbed to my feet and called out to her, halting her manic circling. "Come on, pretty girl. We're going for a ride in the car."

She shot out of the room and barreled down the stairs to the front door.

LaLee gave one last glance in Caphy's direction and then leaped gracefully back to the bed, climbing back into my suitcase with a final glare in my direction.

I shook my head. "You can have the suitcase for another hour or so. Then, I'm going to be unpacking. And you're going to have to find another place to sleep."

"Yowl!" the cranky cat responded. Something told me I wasn't getting her out of that bag without a few claw tracks on my arms.

Fun times.

***

I was starting to worry I'd missed a turn or something when I drove up a hill, took a curve, and finally saw the lights of several police cars in the distance. I stopped my Jeep behind Hal's big Escalade and clipped Caphy's leash to her collar. The pitty was already warbling with excitement and bouncing in her seat.

I followed her line of sight and saw my PI heading our way.

"Who's coming to see you?" I asked my excited Pitbull.

Caphy whined and lunged at the side window, her muscular tail flailing the leather seatback.

I laughed. My sweet pibl loved herself some Hal Amity. Opening my door, I'd barely gotten one sneakered foot on the ground before Caphy shoved past me and strained at the end of her leash to reach Hal. I knew how she felt. I generally strained to get near him too.

Six feet four inches tall, with thick, shiny black hair that was swept straight back from a wide, unlined brow and curled softly against his muscular neck, Hal was a Greek god in a close-fitting black tee, stylishly aged jeans, and scuffed brown boots.

Thick black lashes framed his dark green eyes and his

wide mouth was full and kissable. He had a square jaw with a dimple in the center and broad shoulders that strained the round-necked tee shirt. His only visible flaw was the razor-thin scar that ran from just in front of his left ear to the corner of his eye. I'd asked him about the scar once, but he'd been vague. I had a feeling it was the result of a situation that had scarred him on the inside more than what was visible. He clearly didn't want to talk about it.

Which made me want to know all the more.

"Hey, Beauty," Hal said, crouching down to scratch my dog's floppy ears. He looked up at me. "Sorry to drag you out here, but we have a dilemma we thought our girl could solve."

I nodded, scanning the area. There was a small, muddy, and severely damaged sedan parked cattywampus across the grass, several yards from the road. There was a messy trail of tire tracks in the wet grass, where it appeared the car got stuck in the mud and dug in, slipping and sliding.

A distance away from the abandoned car, something lay on the ground covered in a thin blanket.

"What happened?" I asked, lowering my voice. "Is that a body?"

Hal sighed. "Unfortunately. We appear to have a vehicular homicide. But nothing is adding up." He threw a look toward the cluster of police cars and I noticed a pair of skinny legs sticking out of the back seat of one of them. Deputy Kim Schmidt appeared to be asking the person who owned the legs questions, jotting notes and nodding her head. Whoever was inside the car, he or she was wrapped in a blanket like the one covering the corpse, and looked about as muddy as the abandoned car. "Who's that?"

Hal sighed, the skin around his eyes tightening. "*That* is our resident sociopath."

My eyes went wide. "Shulz?"

George Shulz was Deer Hollow's only lawyer. He maintained the arrogance and disdain of the most reprehensible of his peers, but also worked under the self-proclaimed mantle of sociopathy. Shulz was sans all real human emotion or filters, and he was pleased to be that way.

For the rest of us, the trait moved him well beyond annoying and into hurtful territory.

The first nigglings of worry stirred in my middle. "Why did Arno call you in?"

Hal's gaze suddenly didn't seem able to meet mine. He scratched Caphy's scruff and stared off into the distance.

"Hal?" I let my growing discomfort thread my voice.

He sighed. "Shulz wants Amity Investigations to find the person responsible for all this." He swung his arm to indicate the car and the body.

Discomfort swelled into horror. "You're working for Shulz?" I didn't like the dolphin-like pitch of my voice but I didn't seem able to contain it. "Have you lost your mind?"

Hal turned an angry gaze my way and I flung up a hand, palm out. "I apologize. That didn't come out the way I'd intended. What I meant was, do you really think that's a good idea?"

Hal studied me for a long moment. My heart thudded too fast in my chest. The last thing I wanted was for George Shulz to, even inadvertently, cause a rift between me and my PI.

Finally, he looked away. "I haven't agreed to it yet. I know it would be stupid. The man's a demon."

I nodded, agreeing completely with the sentiment. Not in a euphemistic way. No. I really believed Shulz was a demon from the fiery pits of Hades. Hey, if I believed in God, and I did, then it only made sense the devil existed too.

Shulz was a perfect advocate for the devil. So...demon he was. "But you're considering it, aren't you?"

"Only because Arno asked me to."

I let my brows rise.

"It's the election. He's worried Shulz will use his connections in the legal world to cause problems for him."

"Why on earth would he be worried about that?" I asked.

"Because Shulz told him, *I'll use my connections in the legal world to cause problems for you if you don't get me Amity.*"

I pulled air into my lungs and released it in a frustrated rush. "What kind of problems?"

"Shulz has threatened to make a series of ads featuring high-powered lawyers from Indianapolis, to fling innuendo and plant doubts about Arno's role in the Mayor Robb mess."

Our former mayor had gotten mixed up in a kidnapping and murder case that had dragged our former sheriff down with him. Deservedly so.

But Arno hadn't had anything to do with it, except that it had fallen into his lap to clean up.

It was the reason Deputy Sheriff Arno Willager, a darn good cop and my childhood friend, was currently running for Sheriff. A cynic might believe that, since Arno stood to gain from Sheriff Mulhern's ouster, he could very well have framed the sheriff to get his job. The fact that Arno worked that case made the accusation even more plausible. That was, if you didn't know that Arno Willager was the most decent, honest person one could possibly find.

"Arno doesn't have anything to worry about," I told Hal. "Nobody who knows him would believe he did anything wrong."

"Yeah," Hal agreed. "Unfortunately, not everybody who will be voting for Arno really knows him."

"Amity!" The voice hailing my PI from across the grass belonged to none other than Deputy Arno Willager himself. When we looked his way, he motioned for us to join him near the body.

I didn't need to encourage my dog to follow, she leaped ahead of us as soon as we started walking. If I didn't know her better, I'd be concerned she was trying to get closer to the body to check it out. But I suspected her love-filled gaze was focused more on the deputy sheriff than the body he was overseeing.

Arno smiled when he saw the pibl straining on her leash to get to him. "There she is, the girl of the hour." Arno bent to scratch my pibl under the chin and got a wet swipe of her tongue across his cheek for his efforts. "You ready to do some work, girl?"

"What's going on?" I asked the two men. "What did you want Caphy to do?"

Arno turned his intense brown gaze in my direction. A gentle breeze caught in his longish blond hair as he straightened. Standing next to Hal, his six-foot two-inch frame looked smaller than it was. However, with his lean frame, narrow hips, and broad shoulders, Arno was anything but small. He gave me his worried face, which consisted of two indented lines in the space between his dense golden eyebrows. "Amity didn't tell you?"

"We hadn't gotten around to that," Hal admitted. "We got hung up on my potential client."

I gave Arno a look and he shook his head, putting hands to hips and trying to look intimidating. He usually had no trouble looking menacing, but I'd known him since grade school so he had a harder time making my knees quake. "I asked him to consider taking the Shulz case as a favor," Arno said. His tone was stern, but there was something almost vulnerable in his eyes.

"I don't believe you're really afraid of Shulz's threats," I told my friend.

Arno crossed his arms over his chest, the twin lines deepening on a frown. "Let's just put it this way. I don't believe, ultimately, that his lies would hurt my career. But I don't see why I should have to deal with them, given that I think he's innocent."

Silence pulsed between us at his admission. Hal shifted from foot to foot, seemingly discombobulated by Arno's disclosure. I was pretty sure my eyebrows were tickling my hairline. Even Caphy cocked her head in question.

"How is that possible?" I asked, too loudly. I lowered my voice after drawing Deputy Schmidt's speculative gaze. "Shulz admits that he's a sociopath. You have a victim and you have Shulz in the vicinity." I glanced at the car. "That's Shulz's car, right?"

"It is."

"Then how?"

Arno glanced toward Shulz. "I'll explain later. Right now, the Pitbull has another corpse to find."

ALSO BY SAM CHEEVER

If you enjoyed **Distinguished Bumpkin**, you might also enjoy these other fun mystery series by Sam. To find out more, visit the **BOOKS** page at www.samcheever.com:

Country Cousin Mysteries (For more fun adventures with Joey and Caphy!)

Grave Theatrics Cozy Mysteries

Silver Hills Cozy Mysteries

Gainfully Employed Mysteries

Honeybun Heat Series

Mature Magic Paranormal Women's Fiction

Enchanting Inquiries Paranormal Cozy Mysteries

Yesterday's Paranormal Mysteries

Reluctant Familiar Paranormal Mysteries

ABOUT THE AUTHOR

USA Today and Wall Street Journal Bestselling Author Sam Cheever writes mystery and suspense, creating stories that draw you in and keep you eagerly turning pages. Known for writing great characters, snappy dialogue, and unique and exhilarating stories, Sam is the award-winning author of 100+ books.

To learn more about Sam and her work, visit her at one of her online hotspots:
www.samcheever.com
samcheever@samcheever.com